Brother Elephant

Brother Elephant

A story about a girl and an elephant in Africa

DOUGLAS WARD

authorHOUSE®

AuthorHouse™
1663 Liberty Drive
Bloomington, IN 47403
www.authorhouse.com
Phone: 1-800-839-8640

First published by AuthorHouse   07/14/2011

ISBN: 978-1-4567-8098-2 (sc)
ISBN: 978-1-4567-8099-9 (ebk)

Printed in the United States of America

CONTENTS

1. Erica Meets Martin

As Erica runs across the sandy parking area to the radio shack, she regrets not slipping on her sandals. The ground is so hot it scorches the soles of her feet. "Serves you right," she thinks, considering herself lucky her dad isn't there to tick her off about not wearing her hat and shoes.

"Chiredza Station this is Chiredza Mobile One, do you read?" the volume is set loud so she can hear incoming traffic from the cottage, and she turns it down as she picks up the handset.

"Mobile One, Chiredza Station, hi Dad, what's up?"

Erica's father, Rob Granger, is Chief Warden for the Chiredza National Park in Zambesia, several thousand square kilometres of dense bush, soaring mountains and grassy plains. Home to dozens of species of African wildlife, but recently under pressure from organised poaching gangs, the park has had a good record in controlling the illegal trade. He has gained the confidence of villagers bordering the reserve, including them in the benefits generated by the park. They are quick to inform game guards of new tracks or sightings of strangers in the area.

"I am at Chief Chapoto's village, he sends salaams and asks if you are married yet, over."

"Da-aad! Tell him I'm only twelve, well, nearly thirteen . . ."

"I think he thinks that's a good age to settle down and have babies," said her father with a chuckle. "Okay, Erica, just checking in, we'll be back tomorrow about noon. Are you alright there?"

"Yes, quite fine—Wilson is keeping an eye on me and cooking up his usual stodge." she replied.

"Well, be careful we still haven't found out where that cobra has set up home. Make sure you wear your shoes and hat. Over and out."

1

Erica replaces the handset after saying goodbye and smiles to herself. She and her dad are more friends than father and daughter, although she still has to toe the line. On most things.

Since her mother died of malaria when she was only three, Erica has lived with her father at the ranger station during the holidays and with her aunt Fran in Rafinga for the weeks during school terms. She has become a bit of a tomboy despite her slim build, almond-shaped deep brown eyes set above high cheekbones and expressive lips always seeming to be on the verge of a smile. Her hair which should have been light brown, is burnt honey blonde by the sun. She wears it short, not wanting to waste time brushing it. Ngubane, the Senior Warden under her dad, is her friend and has taught her the ways of the bush and of his tribe. He has also been away with her father on border fence patrol for the past four days, and the station is empty apart from Erica, Wilson the wizened little cook, Chimemwe the office assistant, and Mufara, a new arrival to replace their retired vehicle mechanic. Mufara is a bit grumpy and distant and Erica thinks he does not like being stationed so far from town.

The game guards and their families have their own little village a few hundred meters away, a cluster of neat cottages. Some of the older children go to the same school as Erica, and they often play together during the holidays, but they are on a school choir competition in the city for two weeks, and Erica is comfortable being by herself. She is busy with a study on Meerkats, the amusing little creatures that abound around the station, living in a maze of family burrows and foraging for delicacies like scorpions and centipedes during the day. A system of sentries keeps watch for the hawks and snakes that like to snack on the curious rodents, and each burrow has a nursery run by the younger females who take care of the babies, never venturing too far from the entrance. She has been recording their behaviour and taking photographs, storing the data on her laptop computer. With the help of her dad, who has a doctorate in biology, she is putting her research into a paper that will fulfil her school's requirement for a holiday project and in a small way she hopes, prepare her for university. Erica is not sure what she wants to do, but knows that it will have something to do with the bush and the animals she loves.

As the afternoon shadows lengthened and the heat came off the day, Erica decided to go for a walk towards her favourite kopje, a granite outcrop with acacia and fig trees spreading over huge rounded boulders. Dozens of dassie, the rock rabbit or hyrax, live here, their presence marked by the white streaks of their waste. There is often a black eagle patiently soaring above the ridge, waiting for a young or unwary dassie to step into danger and his swooping talons. Putting on shoes, grabbing a tatty old hat and her notebook, Erica set out, calling to Wilson as she passed the kitchen that she would be back before dark.

"You pasop now, missie Erica. Watch out for the Tokoloshe!"

The Tokoloshe is an imp that takes people away in the night, unless you put your bed legs up on bricks or tin cans, the only known remedy. Erica rates the Tokoloshe with Father Christmas and the Easter Bunny, both good for the gifts they bring, but . . .

As she strode down the path leading towards the hill, Erica made a note of the spoor she saw along the way. There was the dainty print of a tiny dik-dik, the smallest antelope of all, and crossing at right angles, the dog-like pads of a jackal. Beetle tracks, ant trails and kangaroo rat prints—a veritable story book written in sand of a day in the life of the bush. The slightly ominous continuous weaving track of a puff adder made her suddenly more alert, even as she realised it was many hours old, already marked with ant lion traps, the perfect little cone-shaped pits built to collapse as insects blundered into them, alerting the ant lion who would rear out of the sand with strong pincers and drag his prey under in the wink of an eye. Erica liked to tease them by gently brushing the side of the traps with a slender blade of grass, watching them leap out and grab the stem, refusing to let go even when dangled in the air. As soon as they realised this was a vegetarian offering and not a tasty insect, they would let go and furiously burrow back under the sand, starting another trap and no doubt grumpily muttering to themselves.

Climbing easily to the top of the kopje, Erica settled down on her favourite rock, a massive granite monolith shaped like a whale with its tail rearing out of the water. Lichen covered one side of the rock, where most of the rain came from, orange, green and light grey, and amongst the lichen she found her amusing friends, the rock lizards. Coloured in the hues of the lichen and stone, they were almost invisible until they moved, but as they were inquisitive and always hungry, they were easy to spot. Erica always brought them some little scraps from the kitchen, and they gathered around her expectantly, bobbing heads and flicking tails. They were completely fearless, darting in to snatch tiny morsels from her fingers, but never biting or scratching, and when the feast was over, they retreated to their patches of sun or shade like well-behaved dinner guests.

Erica eased her back against the cool smooth bark of a wild fig tree and made some sketches of the closest lizard, chewing on the back end of the pencil between glances at the cheeky fellow. The afternoon was warm, the shade cool, the tree trunk just right, and she felt her eyelids drooping. A nap wouldn't hurt, she thought to herself as the notebook slid from her fingers, momentarily startling the lizard whose portrait was not quite finished. A slight snore escaped her lips before her breathing settled into a contented rhythm and she slid down into a more comfortable position.

A deep voice, seeming to come almost from within her, woke Erica with a start.

"Excuse me. Hey you. Wakey-wakey. C'mon, girl . . . ." She sat up and looked around, not seeing anything at first. "Down here, nitwit, are you blind as well as semi-conscious?"

Creeping to the edge of her rock, Erica peered over the side and almost fell off the edge in surprise. No more than a few feet away, a hairy-lipped trunk waved in front of her face. Attached to the other end of the trunk was a very large elephant. Attached to the elephant were two enormous curving tusks, huge flapping ears and small but bright brown eyes framed by long dark lashes.

"Are . . . are you talking to me?" she faltered, thinking at the same time how stupid that sounded. Elephants don't talk English, they talk Elephant, and they don't talk to people, just crush them into flattened pancakes now and then.

"Who d'you think I'm talking to, that moron of a lizard?" rumbled the elephant, flicking the tip of his trunk contemptuously at the wide-eyed reptile who promptly disappeared.

"OK, I get it, I know what's going on here. I'm having a little dream, that's all. It'll soon be over. I'll just lie down again . . ." Erica started to curl up into a little ball, but a prod from the tip of the elephant's trunk put paid to her theory.

"Nope. Nopety nopety nope. I am as real as the mole on your butt and we need to talk."

4

"What! How did you know about my mole?" Erica leapt to her feet, fists clenched and anger colouring her face. "Did you look while I was sleeping, you bloody pervert?"

"Calm down, it's a longish story, but you will understand when I tell you," the huge animal almost seemed contrite as he tried to calm her down.

"I knew you when you were a baby, and you were so small you probably don't remember anything about me. I am your brother. Well, I guess really your foster brother . . ."

"Not only are you a pervert but a big fat liar as well," blurted Erica. "We are so not having this conversation, and I still don't believe you are real. I'll soon wake up and go home . . ."

A gusty sigh escaped the gently waving trunk.

"Alright, let me explain. I was an orphan elephant from a poaching incident in the reserve. Your dad brought me home, not expecting me to live. I was so small and there are few chances of survival of our kind without our own mother's milk. Your mother took me under her wing and stayed awake for days on end trying different milk formulas that would stay down. I guess I came close to death now and then, and I was so sad about my mum and family I wasn't sure I wanted to live. Then your mother introduced you to me, just a little pink bundle of waving toes and fingers (and a mole on the bottom), and I found I had something to look forward to each day, you crawling around me and playing with me without fear or anger. I started to get better and stronger and soon recovered completely."

"But, how are you talking to me?" Erica asked. "I don't see your lips moving, either your mouth or the end of your trunk. Where is your voice coming from?"

"Ah, well, that takes a bit of scientific explaining and I don't really have the time right now . . ." said the elephant, scuffing one large foot in the dust.

"Aha! You have no idea, do you? So this really is a dream. I'm off again, bye."

"No, no, it's just that even we who communicate like this don't understand it all. Amongst ourselves, we use a deep vibrating rumble way beyond your voice range that we can hear or feel over many miles—like a low frequency radio signal?" he seemed anxious to persuade her.

"So, now you also know about radio as well—quite the accomplished pachyderm. This is unreal. You are unreal."

"I guess what happened was that I came to think of your mother as my mother, and we had a way of communicating that went beyond words. I would think or visualise a thought and project it towards her, and at first, she would just turn towards me with a puzzled look, as if I had farted or something." Erica could not stifle a giggle at that . . ." but, after a while she would understand exactly what I was trying to say, whether it was 'food' or 'love' or 'want Erica.' Before your mother died (when I also wanted to die, by the way) we had developed our communication to the same level that you and I now have. You may not remember me, but you were also part of our growing language skill—we used to chat, even if it was baby talk. Your mother had no boundaries—she would talk to me about anything and explain things patiently. Your dad was away a lot in those days, so the secret was ours alone . . ." the elephant seemed drained by the effort and lowered his massive head. "I really loved your mom, and it devastated me when she was gone. Your father was heart-broken, and he had no time to think that I needed him as badly as you did at that time. I was fully weaned by then, and was returned to the bush, meeting up with the remnants of my herd which recognised and took me back in, teaching me the ways of my species. I taught some of them how to communicate with humans, but our herd leaders, the bulls and senior cows, saw only bad things in people. We had been hunted, shot at, fenced in, herded out, darted and drugged, had idiotic tourists driving right up to us—you name it, we have been there, had that done to us . . ."

Erica started to believe that this might not be a dream, but decided that pinching herself was not going to work, because if you pinch yourself when you are dreaming, how do you know whether you have really pinched yourself? She decided to give it a go anyway.

"Ow! That hurt!" she blurted.

"What, what, I didn't do anything!" said the elephant, stepping back rapidly with his trunk defensively raised.

"Wasn't you, it was me," said Erica, rubbing the red mark on her forearm ruefully.

"I think it's about time for formal introductions—I know you are thinking of me as 'elephant', but I do have a name. I know yours of course," rumbled the grey giant. "My name is Cholmondely Hugh-Jefferson Granger, pleased to meet you."

Erica's jaw dropped so far she thought it might have dislocated.

"Just kidding!" wheezed the elephant, closing his eyes and shaking with what appeared to be laughter. "Actually it's Spongebob Greypants . . . ."

"Oh, just tell me your name before the sun goes down!" Erica grated. "It's Martin." said the elephant quietly, once again shuffling a dustbin-lid-sized foot in the dusty ground.

"Martin? Martin? What kind of name is that for an elephant," Erica hooted, dancing around in a little circle.

"Well, actually, your mother named me. I think she wanted to have a son after you, and had already picked that name . . ."

"Oh, well, in that case, I suppose it's not so bad," Erica allowed. "OK, Martin, I'm maybe starting to believe this is not a dream, or if it is one, it's pretty darn lifelike, if totally unreal, off the wall and downright strange, but why now, after all these years? Why didn't you tell me years ago I had a . . . brother?"

Erica had climbed down off her rock and stood in front of Martin, his tusks almost encircling her.

"Can I touch you?" she asked quietly.

With a low rumble, Martin pushed his trunk forward until it touched her hand. She stroked the coarse hair and tough wrinkled skin. He explored her face with the smooth and supple lips of his trunk, breathing gently, inhaling her scent. They stood like that for what seemed like an eternity.

"When I left the human herd, I saw no point in coming back or trying to be something I'm not. I am an elephant and I need the love and security of my own kind. I would be an oddity in your world, something that people would come and point at and take pictures of—'The Human Elephant' or something like that. My herd seniors also forbade me to make contact, seeing only the bad side of your people. Oh, they know your father cares for them and protects them, and they would never hurt him, but there are many humans who only see us as an ivory ornament or meat, or leather briefcases or fly whisks or footstools . . ." Martin went on, "I thought of you often, and also of our mother, and I have kept an eye on you from a distance. When you thought you were just watching another herd of elephant, you would never have noticed me amongst the others, watching you just as intently."

"So, what has happened now, to change your mind?" asked Erica.

"We are facing great danger and need your help, little Sister," said Martin, looking down at her gravely. "Ivory is in short supply, the Chinese are paying top dollar, and to a local poacher, what must seem a king's ransom makes the risk of killing us inside a protected reserve worth the risk. We notice the movement of strangers in the area, smell the sour scent of the hunters and see their spoor as they track us up and down the valleys, marking the spots where they can find us and ambush us when your father or his rangers are elsewhere."

"But how would they know where the rangers are, or not?" asked Erica.

"Well, that is the real problem—there is a spy in your camp who reports all staff movements to someone", muttered Martin. "I heard some poachers around a fire at night talking about their contact on the inside and how they would soon be able to operate freely when their system has been tested."

"That's impossible!" said Erica. "All our staff are good and honest people. Some of them are even reformed poachers who have seen the error of their ways. They would defend your lives with their own."

"I'm afraid not, Erica. There is someone there who knows everything, has regular contact with the criminals, and feels nothing for our future, only for money."

Erica scanned through the faces of the people she knew in her mind's eye, but nobody stood out, only her friends and the ways in which they accepted her as one of their own.

"I can't think of anyone who would do that," she muttered almost to herself.

"It's not easy to believe there is a traitor amongst the people you love, but we are sure there is someone who is an enemy to all of us," Martin replied quietly.

He looked down at her fondly, resenting the fact that it was a dirty secret that had brought them back together, and regretting the lost years.

"I'll speak to my dad and tell him what you said—he needs to know," said Erica, scrambling back up the rock to retrieve her notebook and pencil.

"Hmm, I think you may have a few problems convincing him you have been having a bush conference with an elephant who speaks English . . ."

"Yes, you are probably right—he might ship me off for observation at a nice quiet hospital somewhere," giggled Erica. "He already thinks I'm a bit odd with all my chatting to Meerkats, injured birds and orphaned monkeys, and this would just top it for him! But, I'll think of something—we can't allow this to happen."

"OK," said Martin, "time for you to be getting back—it's getting towards evening. Let's meet here every few days and see what happens. I will call you long-distance, something like a 'trunk call'. You must be careful when you are looking for clues around the camp. These people are dangerous and will stop at nothing. Do absolutely nothing that would raise suspicion."

What he did not say was that he was scared of having her hurt, or worse, and having second thoughts about involving her in this business at all.

"Remember, I can now also sense what you are thinking, as much as you can me," said Erica. "Don't worry, I will be careful and take things one step at a time. And by the way, I got your weak pun about the trunk call. Ha ha."

Even as she said the words, she was wondering how to sneak around the camp asking questions without raising suspicion, or at least curiosity. Oh, they were all used to her endless questions about birds and insects and where did babies come from and what star is that and how does that work and . . . but this was different. She was possibly going to accuse someone she had known for years of being a thief, a poacher and maybe worse.

2. People Under Suspicion

Erica got back through the gates of the camp fence just before sundown, much to the chagrin of Wilson who always thought girls should be at home sewing or at least helping him peel vegetables in the kitchen, not gallivanting around in the bush.

"Ai missy Erica!" he complained "I thought you had been eaten by lions and your daddy would feed *me* to the hyena . . ."

Erica gave him a quick peck on the cheek before going to wash her hands, leaving him sputtering and smiling at the same time. Dinner was certainly not stodge despite her comments to her dad, and Wilson had set up a table for one under her favourite tree just outside the kitchen, facing the setting sun and the distant mountains. Impala fillets and fresh green vegetables garnished with parsley, and hot runny custard over sponge cake for dessert, life could be worse. Martin was out there somewhere, she thought to herself. So big, so powerful and yet so vulnerable to man's greed and a piece of flying lead weighing about an ounce. What am I to do to help? After helping Wilson with the clearing and washing up, Erica had a cool shower and changed into an old t-shirt and boxers. Sitting down at her laptop at the work station in her study, she brought up her research notes and created a new folder, assuming that few people would know where to look for her thoughts on who the informer might be.

Erica sat and thought for a while, trying to order her thoughts, then decided to list every person in the camp and eliminate those she was sure could not be involved. Next to each person she would list their job, length of service in the department, personal data as far as she knew it, and leave space for more notes as she went along. Of the twenty-four men and women working in the camp, her father,

10

Ngubane, Wilson and she herself could be safely removed, leaving twenty potential suspects.

"Why not Ngubane?" she asked herself. "Because I'd die if it was him", she answered herself. And Wilson had been with the family all her life, a wise dithering old uncle who would not hurt a fly. As she listed every person, their faces and characteristics flashed in front of her.

Tswane, head tracker and senior game guard. He had been in the department for more than twenty years and would be retiring next year. Maybe he needs more than his pension will pay. But his face is so honest and open, and he always seems happy. Surely not Tswane. And his wife Chimemwe, she did odd work in the office, filing and cleaning up. She was a jolly matron, shaped somewhat like a series of basketballs placed on top of each other. She and her whippet-lean husband made an unlikely but loving couple.

"Hmmm. I'll rate them 'Probably not'."

By the time Erica had listed half of the staff, her eyelids were drooping and she was no closer to finding a suspect. Naming the folder 'Meerkat Mischief', she shut down and went to bed, reflecting on the events of this special day, still not sure that they had happened at all. Her dreams were punctuated by the distant rumble of a lion and answering giggle of a scavenging hyena.

Waking with the dawn as usual, Erica yawned, stretched and ambled out to watch the sun rise, listening to Wilson clattering around in the kitchen on the other side of the yard as he prepared tea and toast for her. A quick visit to the bathroom, an even quicker tidy up of her bed, shorts and t-shirt on, and Erica was ready for her day. Giving Wilson a cheery 'good morning' she sat down to her tea, carefully stealing a few crusts of toast and jam for her meerkat family, who would be waiting for her, standing high on back legs, noses sniffing, alert eyes on the skies for hawks and on the ground for snakes. After spending an hour with them, taking some good pictures with her digital camera and making more notes on their behaviour, Erica returned to her investigation file and continued listing the staff.

Viwemi, Richard, Bhigane, Kondwani, Chawezi, Aaron, Bongane. The list went on, and she felt bad prying into their lives, and doubting people she considered to be family. She went through the personal files in the locked filing cabinet in her father's office, getting information she did not have in her head.

She was buried deep in thought when she was surprised by Mufara the mechanic, who walked into the office unannounced, wiping his hands on a piece of cotton waste.

"When is your father coming back?" was his short question, as he twisted his head in an attempt to see what she was reading at her father's desk. "I need more SAE30 oil and some injectors for the tractor."

Erica casually drew some maps and other papers over the files and notebook on the desk and told Mufara that her father was on the way back and that she would let him know as soon as he came in.

"Great." She muttered to herself. "First day on the job as ace investigator and I'm caught raiding the personal files . . ."

She hoped that he had not seen the files or what they meant, and carried on completing her list. When she eventually came to Mufara, who was last on her list as he was the newest arrival, she realised that he in fact could be the prime suspect. He was new, largely unknown to anyone in the camp, had access to information, went to town at least once a week for errands and seemed unhappy to be here. She also knew he had a mobile phone, which while not working in the camp, could pick up a signal by climbing 'Erica's Kopje' and standing on the topmost rock. A few of the staff had got themselves mobiles, and her dad had one for when he was in town for meetings, but they were still a bit of a novelty in this part of the world. She also realised that he could have just filled out a requisition form for the things he wanted, and left it for her father to sign so he could get them from the government depot in town on his next trip.

"He must have seen me through the window, working in Dad's office and wanted to know what I was doing", she thought to herself. "Well, Mr Mufara, I've got my eye on you as well, so be afraid. Be very afraid."

With that bit of bravado out of the way, Erica replaced the files and locking up, returning the keys to their hiding place on top of the door frame. After entering the new information into her computer and updating the files, Erica printed the lists so she could read them properly and make notes, eliminating those she felt were incapable of betraying everything the reserve stood for. She tore the compromising pages out of her notebook and flushed them down the toilet, making sure they all disappeared.

"Thank goodness for spy movies," she thought to herself. "Where else would I have learned the trade? All I need now are a few hidden cameras, some directional microphones, a satellite tracking device, sexy overcoat to hide my trusty Walther PPK and I'll really be in business. Riiiiight! . . ."

She hid the two printed pages in plain sight in her school project folder, after scribbling school notes on the back of the pages and placing them printed face towards each other in a clear folder pocket, so that only the pencilled notes were apparent when leafing through the file.

Erica heard the low growl of the Land Rover long before it emerged from the tree line a mile from the station. She also recognised the distinct sound of her dad's truck, a mixture of rattles and squeaks, legacy of a lifetime on bad roads, choking dust and penetrating mud. She ran to the gate to open it before Wilson got there, waving her father and Ngubane through with her hat and a deep bow, and then giving the three game guards hanging on the back of the truck a thumbs-up as they went past. They all waved back and smiled through dust-rimed faces, looking forward to a shower, change of clothes, and no doubt a cold beer with some home-cooked food. They tumbled off the back, grabbing their rifles and packs, saluting Erica's dad before hurrying off to the guard's village.

"Well done, lads," said her dad "I know we didn't catch them this time, but we were close. Better luck next time . . ."

One of the guards, Kondwani, turned back and said evenly "I don't think it is luck Mr. Rob, I think there is bad medicine out there. Every time we think we have them, they disappear like smoke in the wind, as if they know exactly where we are coming from. Something is not right . . ."

Granger studied him for a moment. He had been having the same thoughts. There was something different about this band of poachers—they did seem to be able to stay one step ahead of the patrols all the time, even with information coming in from the surrounding villages. What was strange was that they were not killing any game, just moving about the reserve, and if they did catch up with them the worst penalty would be a small fine for trespassing, and maybe some attention from the Police if they were caught with unregistered firearms. The problem with the law was that you had to catch them in the act of killing or in possession of the ivory, wire traps or other banned products, not very reassuring for the elephants, which had to be dead to benefit from the ruling!

It was also very dangerous for the department staff, who had been fired on in the past when trying to arrest poachers. It had turned almost into a low-level war, with one side hampered by rules and regulations, lack of resources and people, and the other emboldened with huge rewards for a few days work.

"You may be right, Kondwani, but I think the bad medicine is man-made."

Erica noticed new lines etching her father's face, highlighted by the light film of dust which did some duty hiding the grey streaks in his hair. She realised that he was also worried, and Martin's visit, still a dream to her, came sharply into focus.

Putting his arm around her shoulder, waving off Ngubane's offer of help with his canvas bed-roll, Erica's dad walked her toward the cool veranda outside the kitchen and dining area. He dumped his bedroll near the steps and they sat down on the comfortable old deck chairs, putting their feet up on the railing.

"I could murder a steak. And a cold beer. Doesn't much matter in which order. It was rough out there this time. We must have walked forty miles chasing those swine." He smiled at her "But it is always worthwhile knowing my princess is here when I get back."

Erica leaned toward him, squeezed his hand and asked what had happened.

"They just range freely across the reserve and when somehow they know we are on their tracks, they cut the fence and leave. They know we can't pursue them beyond our own borders."

Wilson came hurrying over with a beer for Granger and cool drink for Erica.

"Welcome back Mr Rob, everything okay here, missy Erica good station manager. Lunch ready in ten minutes," with a wink at Erica, Wilson went back to the kitchen.

"I think Kondwani is right, there is something different about this bunch, almost as if they are trying us out, testing our skills, but they are not getting anything for the effort—no killing, no sign that they are even armed."

Ngubane joined them, having dropped off his kit at his cottage and locked their rifles in the safe in the main office. Wilson brought him a beer, and he sighed as he slumped down into the other chair.

"Man, I hope we don't have to walk that far every time we go on patrol. I need new boots, new socks, and I think, new feet. How's the requisition status for new feet?"

Granger smiled at him and retorted, "Okay for you, you're a youngster. I'm getting too old for this business altogether."

Ngubane snorted, knowing his superior was as fit as he was, and probably had more stamina.

"Well, Rob, I'm off. As you know, it is my leave period and my sister is getting married in South Africa. I'm going to shower and pack. Is it okay if Mufara takes me into Rafinga?"

"No problem Ngubane, I'm sorry we were delayed getting back—you should have left for town yesterday. Don't worry about Mufara, I'll take you in myself, I'm sure Erica wouldn't mind a visit to the shops," this with a sidelong glance at Erica, who agreed with a grin and thumbs up.

Ngubane was ready by the time they had eaten and relaxed for a while, and they all climbed into their own somewhat battered but reliable station-wagon, notable not for its speed, but the great air-conditioning which was like a long-awaited gift after the pounding afternoon heat. On the way to the main gate of the reserve, they passed several herds of wildebeest, zebra and impala, and in the distance a small herd of elephants. One of them turned and walked back towards them a few paces, raised his trunk and trumpeted what sounded like a challenge.

"What did I do?" asked Granger in amusement. "We're not even within spitting distance and he wants an argument!"

Erica smiled to herself. She knew it was Martin, letting her know he was around. She even picked up his faint message.

"Be careful, be careful . . ." underlying the sound of Martin's audible voice.

They signed out at the main gatehouse, with a smart salute from Richard who was on gate duty for a week. The game guards all loved this break from the gruelling bush patrols, a time to relax and chat up the ladies from the nearby village, waiting on the side of the road for a lift to town. It was not an onerous job, as the reserve was remote and the tourist season was some way off, in the dryer and cooler winter. It was a time to repair clothing, shine up the boots, read the newspaper dropped off by the delivery truck on its daily run to the north and generally chill out. They still had to man the gate, be there twenty-four hours a day and keep neat records of any entries and exits from the park, maintain a radio schedule with the base and also keep a watchful eye out for suspicious vehicle movements at night, but it was still a prized duty.

Erica's dad paused to offer a young mother and child a lift when Richard told them the baby was ill and the mother was trying to get to the clinic in the town.

"Looks like malaria", said Ngubane, feeling the child's forehead and noting the pale gums and yellowish tint in the eyes. "But, I think she has caught it early enough for the clinic to sort the little tyke out . . ."

They drove onto the main paved road and headed for Rafinga, idly chatting about things, but always coming back to the strange movements of poachers in the park who did not seem to be poaching.

"I think I'll ask for the department helicopter for a week or so," said Granger. "I know it's hellish expensive and the Director will have a conniption, but it may be the only way to get a handle on these guys. We certainly aren't getting close on foot . . ."

Ngubane glanced across at him. "When do you think you'll get it up to the reserve? I'd hate to miss out on some aerial work around our patch. There's nothing like an overhead view of the ground to appreciate what we are up against."

Granger thought for a few seconds, then, "Well, the sooner the better. I'll speak to the boss tonight and see what the bookings are like for the chopper and pilot. I'll give you a call when I have a definite date and try to make it for after you get back."

They entered the outskirts of the town, really just a rural village with the usual collection of filling stations, stores, clinic, veterinary surgery, a rather seedy hotel, a very good restaurant and bakery, a small bank branch, police station and a government transport depot that served the whole region. This was where the spares and fuel for the reserve were drawn, and Erica remembered Mufara's request for some stuff.

"Oh, I forgot to tell you, Dad, but Mufara needed some things and asked when you were coming back. Sorry."

"No bother," he replied, "If it was important enough he would have seen us before we left. I checked the inbox in the office for requisitions before we left, and there was nothing except Wilson's shopping list and a short one from Chimemwe for some stationery."

Erica thought to herself that Mufara's behaviour was more and more suspicious. Why had he not requested the spares he said he needed? Maybe he wants to come to town on his own, and needs the excuse to make the trip, she mused to herself. When she was alone with her father, she would voice her concerns.

They dropped Ngubane off at the bus stop, wishing him safe journey and a happy time with his family. He waved at them as they turned back towards the town centre, slinging his duffel bag across his broad shoulders and striding towards the ticket office.

They dropped the mother and child off at the clinic entrance where she offered a few dollars carefully wrapped in a handkerchief as taxi fare. Erica gently closed the woman's fingers over the money.

"You are going to need it more than us. Go well, Mama."

After doing the shopping and collection of mail from the little post office off the main street, they went into the restaurant for their 'town treat', a meal not cooked by Wilson, with milkshakes and ending with ice cream and chocolate sauce. Erica's aunt Fran was away on holiday in England, and they had done a quick check on her neat little house two streets back from the main road on their way to the restaurant.

Erica's school was a few miles out of town on the main road to the capital, and some of the teachers lived in the staff hostel full time, even during holidays. Her biology teacher was having lunch in the restaurant and smiled broadly when she saw them come in.

"My favourite pupil," she gushed, "And of course my favourite reserve manager."

Erica went red as a beetroot and sat down at another table as soon as she had said hello to Miss Botha, an unfortunately proportioned young woman with a rather wide bottom, and a much smaller top. A long neck supported a face somewhat reminiscent of a horse, and Erica could not help thinking 'giraffe' every time she saw her. That she was a good and dedicated teacher did not help much. And the fact that she was obviously in love with her dad made it doubly, trebly worse. For his part, Erica's dad had no idea what was going on, or if he did, he was hiding it very well.

"Miss Botha, good to see you, I hope you are enjoying your holiday away from the little monsters."

They chatted back and forth, with Miss Botha extracting a promise that the field trip to the reserve by the biology senior classes was still on for the end of the year and so on, 'yadda yadda yadda', Erica willed her father to break it off and come and sit down so they could order, eat and get out. The worst happened. Her dad asked Miss Botha to join them.

"Oh My God," she thought to herself, an hour of this would kill her. As it turned out, she did not die, the food was as good as always and they were back on the road to the reserve by early afternoon. They did not like driving on the roads at night in this area—kudu, the magnificent spiral-horned antelope, had a nasty habit of leaping out of the bush into the headlights of passing cars.

Having lost the opportunity to talk to her dad about Mufara in the restaurant, she now had second thoughts about accusing him without more proof, and decided to let it slip for the time being. They just chatted comfortably about her project, the reserve, her thoughts on which university she'd like to go to. Anything but Miss Botha. Richard signed them back in, and received a pack of batteries for his beloved transistor radio from Erica, who seldom forgot what they all liked to get from town.

"Well, I'm off to bed, pumpkin," said Erica's dad, stretching and yawning. "It's been a long and tiring patrol and I'm bushed. See you in the morning, let's go for stroll then."

He gave her a hug, a kiss and a tickle and went off to his side of the house. They had enjoyed the evening on the veranda with a cup of coffee and home-made crunchies from Wilson's store of goodies, and the night sky chirred with a cicada symphony. Her father had called the Director and extracted a promise for the department helicopter to come out for a week or so when it was available.

Erica still felt awake and went to her study, pulling out her notes and going over her 'suspect list' again and again, making notes and comments alongside the familiar names. She always came back to Mufara, while admitting to herself she was probably biased because he was new and she had not got to know him at all. She decided on a whim to visit the motor workshop and see what she could see. Taking a powerful torch, she padded across the yard and behind the storeroom area to the motor workshop, really just a tin-roofed shed with an inspection pit, tyre repair equipment, compressor, and a small office with a secure storeroom for tools and spares. The office was not locked, as there was little of value to a thief, although there had never been an outside theft at the base in all its history. Any crook willing to cross fifteen miles of bush with wild lion, leopard and elephant to contend with for the sake of a few dollars or an old calculator probably deserved his rewards. If staff members were caught stealing, they knew their jobs were on the line, and Erica's dad had a zero tolerance policy respected by all.

Erica sat down at the desk and scanned the papers neatly stacked in piles for filing, action or pending. On top of the 'out' basket she saw a requisition for the items Mufara had said he needed.

"Hmm. So he did make out the requisition. Maybe just forgot to take it over to the office in time . . ."

She opened the diary, somewhat grubby and oil-stained (it had been around long before Mufara's arrival) and turned to the month of his arrival, flicking through the days up to today's date. There were few entries, just reminders of spares to get and vehicle service mileages, but suddenly an entry from a week earlier caught her eye. Pencilled lightly in the margin was the following code: GN+30700GPP5DAYSEC4. She could make no sense of the note, and copied it onto her wrist with a ball pen before closing the diary and returning it to its original position on the desk.

Once back in her study, Erica quickly copied the message down, scrubbed the number off her wrist and started to study it.

"Government Notice? Doesn't sound right. General Notification? Nope. Gearbox Number? Maybe."

She puzzled over the meaning for a while, until the only thing that made sense appeared to be the 0700, perhaps referring to a time.

"OK, let's separate the 0700 and make it look like this," she muttered to herself, writing down GN+3. 0700. GPP5DAYSEC4. "So, if it refers to a time, and I know the date, also because it was in a diary, and that's when my dad went on park patrol, where do we go from here?"

Suddenly it dawned on her that her father, Ngubane and the three guards had left as usual at seven o' clock sharp on that date, and the code leapt into focus.

"**G**ranger, **N**gubane **plus 3** guards left at **0700** for a **G**eneral **P**ark **P**atrol for **5 Days**." **SEC4** must refer to the map sector of the park, broken up into six distinct zones. There was nothing particularly sinister about the note, but she had a feeling it was important. Maybe Mufara just needed to know where the patrol vehicle would be and when it was coming back in for servicing. Then why list all the members of the patrol and the sector?"

She remembered how lightly the note had been pencilled and realised that there may have been others, hidden in the margins from her casual inspection. Going through her own diary on her laptop, she noted the dates of previous patrols on a scrap of paper, and went back to the workshop.

As she rounded the corner of the stores building, she saw a light on in the office and someone moving around. Drawing a sharp breath, she froze, then edged slowly back around the corner. Heart beating rapidly, she considered running to the house and calling her dad, but immediately told herself not to be silly. This was her home as much as anybody's and she had a right to know what was going on. She peeked around the corner in time to recognise Mufara quietly closing the office door and walking away towards his cottage.

"Well, it is his office and he has every right to be there. But why at nine o' clock in the night? Maybe he forgot a book or something . . ."

She waited for another five minutes, having heard the door to Mufara's cottage close and seen a bedroom light shine dimly through the curtains. Then, moving like a leopard on the hunt, she crept back to the office and gently eased the door open. Shading the torch with one hand, she reached for the diary. Which was not there! Frantically she rummaged around, wondering if she had let it slip off the desk or under some of the documents. But, no, she distinctly remembered putting it squarely back in the middle of the desk where she had found it.

With a sense of foreboding, Erica scurried back to her study, destroyed all her notes and scraps and shut down her computer before going to bed, wondering if she had made a serious miscalculation by raiding Mufara's office. Her dad would give her little sympathy for invading his privacy, even if she told him why she had done it.

She reached out to Martin with her mind and he immediately responded, a vibrating somewhere below her diaphragm, resonating into her brain.

"I'm close by. Do not worry, no one will harm you, little Sister . . ."

"Easy for you to say", she muttered to herself. "You weigh around five tons and are permanently armed to the teeth. With big teeth."

"I heard that," Martin rumbled back. "We might be big, but we are babes in the wood when it comes to the ways man can hurt us . . ."

They exchanged the news that Erica had discovered, or not, as the case seemed to be. Martin said that he was going to stay within a few miles of the station in the future, in case she needed him. The other young bulls would range further and report back to him every few days, and a good coverage of the park should be achieved. They said their goodnights and Erica climbed into her bed, thinking about the day. Her last thoughts before she drifted off were of her mother, She had to look at the photo album now and then to remind her how her mother looked, but she would never forget the love and kindness that surrounded her when her mother was in her life.

3. Mufara

In the early morning's cool and gentle light, Erica walked with her father around the perimeter of the camp, looking at the tracks and signs of animal movement during the night, chatting quietly about this and that.

"Do you think someone in the base may be feeding information on your patrols to the poachers?" she asked suddenly, bringing him back to the frustration of the past weeks.

"Well, much as I hate to think about it, if there is an informant, he or she has to be close to us in order to get accurate information. Every patrol has a pre-determined sector of the park to cover. We cannot just go out randomly and hope to do the job properly. Although, when I think about it, maybe a random pattern *is* the answer . . ." he seemed deep in thought. "But then again, we'd just be wandering around with no idea at all, and hoping on pure chance to stumble over something."

Erica asked him how he planned the patrols, and he described how he and Ngubane would sit down with the maps and patrol diaries and plan the next trip, marking the route on the huge map of the entire park, pasted on the wall in the main office. Each zone was patrolled in rotation, but sometimes they reversed the order to avoid an obvious pattern and to keep the guards alert. The plan was finalised at least three days before they left, allowing time to ensure vehicles, equipment and the men were all available. A briefing before the day of departure was held with the whole patrol group, outlining where they were going, probable overnight campsites and any special instructions. Weapons and ammunition were issued and signed for, and the vehicle packed before evening to ensure an early start. It was Ngubane's responsibility to ensure the VHF radios were charged, enough fuel was on board and that the rations were adequate for the time away. He also made sure that the GPS (Global Positioning System) receiver was in order. This instrument used satellite signals to accurately locate their position on the ground, and also showed their previous movements in perfect detail. The GPS data was downloaded to the main computer and added to the patrol observations data. At the press of a button they could see what animals were seen, with the time, place and date accurately recorded.

"So, what you are saying is that almost anyone with access to the office could know exactly where you are going, what your overnight stops are likely to be, and how long you will be out," asked Erica.

"Yes, but heck, it has not needed to be a state secret, for God's sake. It's just a job that needs to be done, and we have been doing it for years with no problem," he muttered, almost to himself. "Why your sudden interest in this, Erica? Do you know something I don't?" He turned to her, quizzing her with his pale blue eyes.

"Not really," she replied evenly," It's just that I worry about you out there when the odds are against you, and I think Kondwani was right when he said something is going on. It doesn't take a rocket scientist to work out that somebody seems to know how to avoid your patrols. They must either be following you when you should be following them, or they have the information before you even leave the base."

"I'm afraid you are right, girl. Well, from now on, only Ngubane and I, and of course you, will know what the patrol zone is before we leave here. That should complicate any informant's life . . ."

They returned to the veranda of the main cottage for breakfast before Granger went to his office to catch up on the endless paperwork that seemed to cascade from head office and for which he could see little purpose. Erica got back to her research files and started working. The Director called Granger around mid-morning with a confirmation of the helicopter and pilot for a date a week ahead. That would give them time to get jet fuel in drums from town and prepare the guest cottage for the pilot and flight engineer.

"Pity about Ngubane," Granger mused to himself, "He won't be back from leave, but tough luck—the chopper is only available during that time. I'll drop him an SMS in any event, letting him know the dates in case he really wants to come back."

He picked out the message on his seldom-used mobile and whistled for Erica, his well-rehearsed copy of a wood hoopoe.

"You'll never get it right," she teased him as she came into his office. "You sound like a constipated babbler, not a hoopoe".

"Hmm, aren't you the cheeky one," he grinned. "Please would you climb Erica's pimple and send this message to Ngubane. The helicopter is due next Tuesday and he's not going to make it."

Erica took the 'phone, went to get her hat, then trotted all the way to her hill and climbed up to the very top, flipping the mobile open and pressing 'send' whilst gazing around at the beautiful views. The 'phone beeped its cheerful tone to indicate the message had gone, and she slipped it back into her pocket, preparing to climb down. As she started sliding down the first slope, she suddenly noticed a cigarette butt squeezed into a small crack in the granite. Using a twig broken off a nearby acacia she worked the butt out, and with a grimace of distaste straightened it out until she could read the brand name on the filter. Not many people on the base smoked, and she had never seen a butt here, or even around the base. Her dad would go ballistic if he found any garbage, especially cigarette ends lying around. She carefully wrapped it in a Mopani leaf and put it in her pocket.

"Sherlock Holmes on the job," she said to herself. "Just hope I do better than my recent attempts at detecting," thinking of her two close encounters with Mufara.

She had not seen or spoken to Mufara yet, and was in two minds about how to approach him at all.

"What if he saw me in his office and knows I looked in his diary?" she asked herself. "What could he do about it anyway? Report me to my dad, I suppose."

She decided to let things take their course today and handle any encounters as they came up. As she scrambled down the last few rocks to ground level, she knew Martin was there, even though she could not see him.

"Come on out, don't be shy, I won't hurt you," she called softly.

"Yeah, right, do me a favour," he rumbled as he came around the side of the kopje. "I eat babies like you for breakfast, make my day, keep 'em dogies rollin', are you talkin' to ME?" he put on the worst movie bad-guy voices she had ever heard.

"Where on earth did you get those from?" she grinned.

"Our mom used to let me watch videos. Said it would be good for my education. I actually think she got tired of my constant questioning sometimes, and just parked me in front of the television."

The vision of a little elephant sitting on his bottom avidly watching TV was almost too much for Erica, who burst out laughing.

"Well, you need some updating, buddy-boy. Those movies are about a hundred years old. I don't even recognise half of them."

"One must make do with what one has at any given time," Martin replied with a dignified sniff.

They moved into the shade of the massive fig tree, Erica holding Martin's one tusk tip in her hand, feeling its smooth and cool surface, wondering why mankind would rather see this as a carved napkin ring than gracing the head of the biggest land mammal on earth. They chatted for a while, Erica updating Martin on her latest finds and almost-misadventures.

"We have not seen any activity in the park for a few days either," he reported. The poachers seem to be waiting and watching from outside the fence."

She told him about her father's plan to keep the patrol schedules secret until the day of departure, even from the guards who would be going along, and he agreed it would be a good start. She showed him the cigarette butt and he inhaled the scent, knowing he would recognise it anywhere in the future. She warned him about the helicopter, knowing some elephants panicked when the noisy clattering machine swooped over them.

"Thanks for that, Sister, I'll warn them. My old aunt from the breeding herd on the other side of the reserve goes bananas when they fly over. She was darted from a helicopter when she was young, and it was a traumatic experience, although I personally think she is a bit of a drama queen."

They parted with a pat on the shoulder for Martin and a face-feel for Erica by that amazingly gentle trunk.

Erica's dad was just closing the office for lunch when she got back.

"What on earth happened to you? Were you daydreaming out there? You've been gone for nearly two hours, and I was just starting to worry, you Noo-Noo."

She glanced sheepishly at his wristwatch, agreeing that she had been gone a long time.

"Oh, I was just watching the hyrax play and lost track of the time. Sorry." She handed him his mobile 'phone, stood to attention, saluted and said "Mission accomplished, Captain".

They went off for lunch, and afterwards Erica decided to go for a swim in the concrete reservoir that held the emergency water supply for the base. It was deliciously cool and the slightly slimy floor and walls of the dam made her skin turn to goose bumps. Yuk! She floated around until her fingers were wrinkled before climbing out and heading back to her room. She was about to toss her shorts into the laundry hamper when she remembered the cigarette butt. Slapping herself on the forehead with an open palm, she once again reminded herself how bad an investigator she was turning out to be.

"This is not a game, this is not a game, this is . . ." she repeated to herself. She hid the cigarette butt, once again in plain view, on her shelf of bits and pieces: in amongst a hyrax skull, an old cast-off snake skin, coloured pebbles from the river bed, some interesting thorns and dried flowers, the twisted Mopani leaf fitted in perfectly with the display.

"Just hope Dad doesn't find it," she said to herself with a rueful grin. "He'd no doubt think I had taken up smoking and would freak out."

Erica decided to visit Mufara at the workshop, and walked over quickly before she lost both her momentum and courage. She saw him leaning over the engine of the Land Rover, the bonnet removed altogether to make access easier, spanner in one hand and an inspection lamp in the other.

"Hello Mufara, busy as usual?" she sounded false to herself, but Mufara lifted his head out of the engine compartment and replied, quite cheerfully,

"Hello there Erica. Yes, your father sure knows how to make a car work for its living!" He wiped his hands off on the ever-present cotton waste and stepped off the bumper down to ground level. "This old thing is on its last legs, or rather wheels. Even spares are becoming hard to get, it is so old. I am going to recommend to the Director that we scrap it and get your father a new model. They always complain about expenses, but you don't see the department bigwigs in the city driving anything else but the latest 4x4's, even when they probably don't know where the low range selector is . . ."

This was the longest speech she had ever heard from Mufara, and she realised he was intelligent and also had a sense of humour.

"Want a cup of tea?" he asked, "I put the kettle on a few minutes ago and I think I can hear it whistling."

"Sure, that would great. Tell you what, let me sneak into the kitchen and see if I can raid Wilson's cookie jar before he knows what's happening."

She strolled nonchalantly over, and saw Wilson hanging towels on the washing line strung between two trees in the back garden of the kitchen. She snuck into the pantry and grabbed a handful of freshly-baked biscuits from the jar and made a dash for the door, making it just as Wilson came in through the back entrance.

"Whew, close thing," she said to herself as she trotted back to the workshop, where Mufara had already set up two cups with milk and sugar standing by. The tea pot, a battered old aluminium camping model, with many dents and a blackened bottom, steamed with the smell of strong Malawi tea. Erica placed the cookies on a clean piece of paper on Mufara's desk, noticing that the diary was back in its original position. She poured the tea for both of them and helped herself to a bit of milk and sugar.

"I think the English say that you are supposed to put the milk in first," observed Mufara, "But I have to admit I have tried it both ways and cannot tell the difference. Strange people, those British."

"Yup," agreed Erica, "My great-grandfather was from England, but since then we have been African, even if we don't meet the skin colour criteria!"

She saw a smile forming on Mufara's normally stoic face and started to feel more comfortable with him, even as he remained her number one suspect.

"But your Aunt Fran, she goes every year to England—is she also an African?" he asked, with one eyebrow raised.

"Well", replied Erica, "Yes and no. You see, her sister went back to England many years ago, and cannot afford to come out here more than once every couple of years, so she tries to make sure they see each other at least once every year. She can afford it, what with owning two of the biggest buildings in Rafinga, as well as the filling station."

Aunt Fran had been left the buildings and garage business by her father, who had invested in Rafinga in its early days when land was cheap and the village consisted of a few rickety tin-sided shops and shacks. The largest supermarket leased the bigger building, and the local government and village administration the other. The service station was managed by a retired farmer from the area, now living in town and needing something to do with his days. He shared the profits with Aunt Fran, and they had been successful business partners for nearly ten years.

"Yes, it is good to maintain family ties," Mufara said, "Even when one has to travel thousands of miles . . ."

"Just like Ngubane," Erica said. "He has had to travel all the way to South Africa to his sister's wedding."

Mufara looked up at that and said, "Oh, I didn't know he had gone South for that. I'm sure he didn't mention it to other staff, but then again, I guess I'm new and not part of the family yet . . ."

Erica also found it a bit odd that Mufara did not know about Ngubane's trip. Family business is normally everybody's business in the small community of the station, but she put it out of her mind as she asked

"So, where do you come from, Mufara? Where are your family ties?"

"Oh, I'm a bit of an anomaly in the extended family business," he smiled, "I am an oddity of an orphan. I was brought up in a Catholic church near Mazimba and went to the church school right up to the time I went to . . ." he paused suddenly and then went on " . . . to a trade school for my mechanics courses."

She was certain he was going to say something else, but the moment was gone.

"I have a girlfriend in the city, but my transfer here is making it difficult. She will not come and live in the bush. She has a good job and a nice little apartment, and I need this job and cannot choose my postings for the time being."

That would explain why he sometimes seemed a bit remote and offish, Erica thought to herself, but something is missing here. Mufara seemed too intelligent to be just a low-level mechanic, or if he was, he was being wasted. She found herself liking him more, despite her reservations and original suspicions, and they chatted about things generally, with Mufara being well read and knowledgeable on many subjects.

"Well, I'd better get back to work. Wouldn't do for the boss's daughter to see me slacking. Thanks for the biscuits, they always taste better stolen than bought . . ." Mufara started tidying up the tea things, but Erica said she would do it and took the tray over to the small wash bay in the workshop to rinse everything, leaving the last biscuits on top of the diary on the desk.

"Well, he had plenty of time to accuse me of prying in his office and reading his diary, but he really did not seem to have any suspicions," she thought to herself. "But he is keeping something back and I need to do some more digging . . ."

Erica had access to the Internet when the generator was running in the base, and when there were few clouds. It was a satellite link and sometimes a bit patchy, but she knew the best times to ask her dad to switch it on so she could check her mail and do on-line research. She popped in to his office and asked him to switch on the wireless connection as the generator had just sputtered to life, a chugging diesel engine in a shed as far away from the main buildings as possible.

"No problem, Hon, done!" he said as he flicked on the power to the main computer and checked his screen. "Good connection today, enjoy . . ."

He returned to his work and Erica went back to her study and entered her queries into the search engine, looking for the trade school Mufara had said he attended. It came up immediately, the M.B. Chanawasa Polytechnic, listing the many courses and wonderful lives graduates would have after signing up with Mr. Chanawasa. Erica thought for a bit, and then typed up a letter, supposedly from the service station in the village, saying that a Mr. Mufara Mangoswene had applied for a job as a mechanic, but had lost his papers. Could they please confirm his attendance, grades and demeanour? She attached the letter to an e-mail to the registrations office address given and sat back, hoping no one would query her right to use her Aunt's business as a cover. Next, she managed to get into the data base for countrywide high school pass results for the last ten years, not a big deal as it was a public record site, but it took her a while to work her way through the forest of information. She knew Mufara's age from the personal records, and could work backward to a span of no more than three years when he should have graduated from high school. It took a few tries, but sure enough on the third go, his name popped up on the screen. She saved and filed the report and exited from the site. Going back to the report, she realised that Mufara had passed at 'A' level with near-perfect grades in all subjects and had automatic university entrance. Even if he was poor, with grades like these he would be offered bursaries and scholarships by the dozen.

"Why, he could have been a doctor or lawyer, but he chooses to get his hands dirty," she muttered to herself. "Curiouser and curiouser."

Suddenly she realised what she had said to herself—'gets his hands dirty'. Mufara's hands were certainly dirty from working on the engine, but not the ingrained dirt that comes with being a mechanic for years. His hands were strong, but almost delicate, like a piano player, with clean and trimmed nails. He always cleaned his hands after every job, and was never without a wad of clean cotton waste.

"So, maybe he's just a hygienic mechanic," she pondered.

Her reverie was broken by the 'ding' of an incoming mail, and she opened it up, surprised to see the Chanawasa Polytechnic had already replied. But, something was amiss. The polite note from the registry office stated with regrets that they had never had a Mr. Mangoswene on their books, was the spelling perhaps incorrect? She sat back, pushing herself away from the desk on her old typist's chair, wondering why he had lied to her. She was sure the spelling was correct—there was a copy of his driver's licence in his file and she had checked it against his other documents.

Erica had often been to the head office of the Wildlife Directorate in the ministry buildings in the city with her father, sometimes waiting for him in the Director's office waiting room while he was busy. She had made friends with the Directors secretary, exchanging news from the reserve with the latest chat and rumours in the Ministry. Her name was Ainu, a bright young lady with good connections in government circles, being related to the President. Erica had corresponded with her a few times by e-mail and now drew her chair up to her desk again and drafted a message. She chatted about trivialities and news for a few sentences, then got down to business. She asked Ainu if she knew of Mufara, a pleasant young man, recently arrived at the station who seemed to have a girlfriend in the city and was not really happy out here, and so on, couching her enquiries in what she hoped was idle curiosity. Drawing a deep breath, she hit the 'send' button and watched the message disappear into thin air. It was no more than fifteen minutes later that a reply came in from Ainu.

"My boss is away for the day, and my work is up to date. I'm glad you mailed, I'm bored to tears! Yes, I do know a little of Mufara. It was quite strange—people on transfer very seldom come for a private interview with the Director, and normally only very senior postings, like your father, would be seen as important enough for this. But, I received a request from Permanent Secretary, (as you know second only to the Deputy Minister) to set up a meeting here with a Mr M Mangoswene a couple of months ago. The PS was there, and some other guys in suits, but they used the conference room and told me they were not to be disturbed. They were only in there for an hour and left quickly, no tea or coffee or anything. I assumed that he was some kind of specialist, like a researcher, talking about funding from WWF or something like that. Did not think much of it at the time, and now you tell me he is a mechanic at your station. You sure we are talking the same person? I am intrigued, little lady of the bundu. Check the spelling and all forenames and come back. I'm off to town for lunch and a hairdo—when the boss is away, the mice will play. Hee hee. Later. Ainu."

"Well, well," muttered Erica to herself, "Mr Mufara is definitely a dark horse, but it now seems he may be a white horse under all of that. "Why would he be important enough for a meeting with the powers that be when he is just going to be fixing clapped-out working vehicles on a remote station?"

She pondered on the mystery for a while, then replied to Ainu that she had double-checked the spelling and provided all Mufara's given names, and also his identification number which was on his driver's licence. She shut down her computer and let her dad know she was finished with the wireless link for the day. He was standing at the big wall map with a wax pencil, making notes on its plastic overlay.

"What's up, princess?" he asked, giving her a red dot right between the eyes with the pencil. "There you go, now you really are a princess, an Indian Rani of the Lower Punjab. Salaams, memsahib . . ."

"Sometimes I wonder about you, father of mine. One minute you are my fifty-something dad and the next you are a naughty boy!"

He grinned and showed her what he was doing, marking off areas that seemed most likely to show results from the aerial survey.

"No point searching the mountain areas—no game, hard access and escape, so probably no poachers. We'll concentrate on the areas around water points, good grazing and known elephant trails, and run the fence line at the beginning and end of every day to look for illegal entry and exit points."

He was transferring the information onto smaller folding maps that the pilot would be using, marking each area with GPS coordinates that the pilot could programme into the helicopters navigation system.

"A long way from the old days when all we had was an old compass and an even more ancient surveyor's theodolite," he said to Erica, who was helping him re-fold and mark each map before slipping them into plastic sleeves.

"Theo-what?" she asked. "Sounds like a Greek shipping tycoon . . ."

"Oh, the ignorance of modern youth. A theodolite, or dumpy level in common terms, is like a small telescope on a tripod with a bubble-levelling platform that allows you to get accurate measurements from one point another by placing graduated poles at intervals, and . . ."

Erica held her hands up, stopping him in mid-stride.

"Too much information, thanks. I think pressing a button on the GPS is a far better way of doing things."

Her father agreed with her, but reminded her that a GPS receiver, radio or satellite was only as good as its batteries, did not like getting wet, dropped or mishandled, and lightning strikes could wipe out every function in a second. They chatted about the amazing accuracy of the modern system, especially for the tracking of game like elephant and lion with what used to be radio collars, now GPS satellite tracking collars, with tiny transmitters and long-life batteries. Selected animals were darted and collared and Granger and his team could download their movements twice a day using software developed by themselves. Apart from the momentary trauma of the darting and being put to sleep for a few minutes, the animals were easy to pinpoint without having to physically track and disturb them, giving a more natural picture of their movements.

"I suppose you could just as easily track people as animals," said Erica. "I have heard that in some places in America, criminals on parole or out on trust have to wear an ankle collar that reports on their movements, or at least warns if they move out of an agreed area."

"Yes, I know about that, and it is exactly the same technology. Even fancy mobile 'phones now have GPS capacity and some people are worried that they can also be transmitters as well as receivers, pinpointing where they are at any time. Be useful for keeping an eye on you!" he chuckled.

Erica thought about it for a few seconds and then said, "Dad, do you think it is possible someone has put a satellite tracking device of some kind on your patrol vehicle? That way, if they had the technology, they'd be able to follow you and plot your movements anywhere."

"Sounds a bit far-fetched, Erica. Not impossible I guess, but the equipment is expensive, and they would have to have access to the vehicle from time to time to fit and check the bug. Then they'd have to have a base to work from, not too far away. On top of that, they'd also have to have good communications by radio or mobile 'phone to report movements to the bad guys."

Erica agreed that it sounded a bit complicated, but mentally filed the conversation to add to her growing dossier. She also resolved to check the patrol vehicle from top to bottom once Mufara had finished servicing it and it was back in the carport near the house, just in case. She finished helping her father sort and fold the maps into the correct order and told him she was going to Erica's Kopje for an afternoon walk.

"OK, take care, be back before sun down. Join me on the veranda for drinks at six . . ." She went to get her hat and walking shoes, binoculars and note book and strolled out of the main gate towards the small hill. Halfway there, she saw someone approaching from the opposite direction, but the sun was behind the person and she could not make out who it was. She was not worried and carried on walking. As they neared, she saw it was Mufara, and he had an angry expression on his face.

"What's the problem Mufara? You look like you just bit into a really sour lemon."

He stopped in front of her, and she saw the mobile 'phone clenched in his right hand, almost like a weapon.

"It's nothing," he muttered. "Just some personal business."

"Oh, I am sorry, Mufara, I didn't think before I opened my big mouth—you just looked so put out and I figured it was something to do with work . . ."

"No. I am the rude one. Sorry I was so short. My girlfriend is not happy with the situation and is talking about us breaking up. I am wondering if she has already found someone else," he said in a subdued voice.

"I think you need to resolve the situation face to face and fast," said Erica firmly. "One thing my parents taught me was never to shy away from problems, but to confront and resolve them, even if the outcome may not be what you want. Why not take some time off and go and see her, try and clear up the issues. Steaming out here is not going to help either of you . . ."

Erica thought to herself that she sounded like an agony aunt from a teen magazine, but Mufara seemed to brighten up a bit and said,

"Erica, you may be a young girl, but you are also wise. I am a man and I need to find out whether this woman is going to be good for me as a wife. If she cannot live without me for a while now, what chance do we have for the future? I'll ask your father for a few days leave and go to town."

"I think my dad might just have some errands for you to run in the city, so I don't imagine you are going to lose too many leave days. I'm off to my hill, are there any more of you guys up there using my private property for making 'phone calls?" She looked at him cheekily.

"No, I was the only one, and the reception was not great anyway—a thunderstorm over Rafinga, I think. And I will make a booking next time." He waved at her as they parted, looking a bit more relaxed than before.

Before he was out of earshot, Erica turned and called back to him, "Mufara, you don't smoke, do you?"

He shaded his eyes against the sun, now in his face, and replied, "No, never have, never will, don't like it. Why?"

"Oh, no big reason, just someone dropped a butt on my hill and I wondered who it might be." Turning again to walk on, she was secretly pleased that he was not the mystery smoker, no matter how innocent that smoker may have been.

Martin picked her up before she reached her hill this time, drifting like a grey ghost out of the heavy Mopani forest, incredibly quiet for an animal of such size. Until his stomach rumbled like a freight train and spoiled the whole effect.

"Pardon," he said, stifling another satisfied belch. "Those Mopani are just at the right stage for munching, and a guy's gotta munch . . ."

They stood close as usual, touching briefly before walking on towards the hill and away from any watching eyes.

"I did check the area out, just that man you stopped and spoke to. There is nobody else around, and he didn't see me. Who was he?" he asked the ace detective.

"That was Mufara, my prime suspect who has turned out to be a real man of mystery. Nothing seems to fit with him, but despite my suspicions I quite like him," she answered.

"Hmm. I also did not pick up any bad vibes apart from some sadness in his aura," said Martin.

They discussed the latest developments and Erica confirmed the helicopter booking, telling him where the search would begin and end so he could pass the word.

"I think it's time for you to learn how to ride an elephant," said Martin suddenly. "One day we may need to cover ground quickly and you need to know what it's like up here, in the air, where it's rare, and most don't have a care . . ."

"Alright, alright, enough with the sales pitch, elephant—tell me how to get up there, where it's rare."

Martin lifted his right knee until it was parallel to the ground and then laid his trunk on the ground in front of Erica.

"Step aboard," he invited her.

She stepped gingerly onto his trunk and held onto a tusk for balance as he slowly lifted it, then moved up onto his knee.

"Well done," he said. "Next step, grab my ear at the top, no not there, closer to my head. There. Just right. Now the trunk again, but a bit higher up."

She stepped onto the thinner part of his trunk, nearer the tip and he boosted her effortlessly up and over his ear and onto his neck.

"Well done!" he called. "All OK back there?"

"Yes fine, except I am facing backwards. Have you done this before?" she shouted back.

"Nope, but there's a first time for everything. We'll get it right. Just turn around and sit on my neck with your legs behind my ears. They will protect you from thorns and stuff." She shuffled around and sat comfortably behind the massive head, legs dangling either side of the wide neck and behind the leathery ears.

"Eeha! Giddyup! Git along now!" she banged her heels against his shoulders and raised her hat high in the air.

"Why am I not surprised?" he murmured. "Everyone wants to be a cowboy. Or girl."

He started ambling off towards the little hill, which appeared even smaller now to Erica, perched up where she felt she was Mistress of the

Universe and Other Things. The motion was comforting, a little like horseback, but softer and a bit more swaying from side to side.

"This is wonderful, Martin. Thank you, I could ride for days up here."

"It's a pleasure, I can hardly feel you up there, are you a mosquito, or what?"

They walked past Erica's Kopje and continued towards the mountains, stopping now and then to look at interesting things. An ant-bear hole recently taken over by a bat-eared fox family, an industrious line of ants on a mission to who knew where, a secretary bird nest, everything seemed new to Erica from her lofty vantage point.

"Home time," said Martin eventually. "I'll take you as close as possible, now hold on while I show you my turn of speed."

He accelerated to a fast run, covering the ground at a deceptively fast pace for the short steps he seemed to take. Erica clung onto the thick ridge at the top of the ears, just like motorcycle handlebars, and shouted with delight at the wind in her face.

"Me, aboard a charging elephant, now that's something to tell my dad!"

Martin abruptly slowed down and moved towards the tree line, just out of sight of the station, where only the water tower showed clearly.

"See you soon, Sis." he said as he lifted her gently down to the ground.

She stroked the front of his trunk and then gave it a hug, just about the only part of an elephant you can get your arms around.

"Take care, Martin. I love you . . ." she walked away into the fading afternoon light and home.

Erica met her dad on the veranda, beating him, she guessed, by a few seconds. Wilson brought them their usual drinks and they completed the ritual by resting their feet up on the rail.

"So, what did you see on your ramble?" her father asked.

"Oh, a bit of this, a bit of that. A new bat-eared fox den, I think with babies—there were some tiny prints around the entrance," she said in an even voice. "No, actually I was riding the back of a stampeding African bull elephant," was what she wanted to say.

"You smell a bit gamey," he said, leaning toward her and making a big production of a sniffing buffalo, flaring his nostrils. "What have you been playing with now?"

Thinking quickly, Erica came up with "I paid a visit to the skins store to check on the pattern of the black-faced impala for my sketches."

The skins store was where all the hides from dead game found or confiscated were kept until transported to town for auction at the Government warehouse.

"Poo. Make sure you have a good shower just now. Smells more like jumbo to me. Were you fooling with the old elephant trophies in there?"

"Well, maybe, just a little," she said, relieved that he had bought her story. One day she would tell him, but not now.

4. NICK

A few days passed with Erica no closer to finding out who might be passing information to the poaching gang. The helicopter had arrived and the pilot and flight engineer were doing some maintenance and checking the maps and intended patrols with her father. Mufara had left for the capital, with a list of things to do for the reserve, using one of the spare vehicles. Ngubane had 'phoned and asked for a pick-up in the village, arriving on the next day's bus, having cut his leave short by a few days.

"I was getting bored anyway, with all that sitting around and drinking beer and talking about cattle . . ."

The station seemed to have fallen back into its normal routine and Erica was enjoying writing up her Meerkat notes, taking her daily walk and meeting up with Martin in the Mopane forest. They would walk and talk and Erica would take rides, now wearing old jeans to stop the prickle from the coarse hair on his neck. Martin confirmed that things were very quiet, with no reports from the young bulls of unusual movements in the park. She was out with him the next morning, following a honey guide to investigate a beehive somewhere in the forest when they heard the clattering roar of the helicopter coming overhead.

"Quick! Jump down, Erica," Martin said, moving towards some taller trees. "It wouldn't do for you to be seen on my back right now."

Erica slid down in her now practiced manner, using his left tusk as a swing bar as she touched the ground and ran for a thicket of bush. The helicopter rushed overhead without pausing and it seemed they had not been seen. Erica could make out the pilot and her father sitting up front, her father in the left seat with binoculars slung around his neck. There was someone in the rear seat, but she could not see who it was.

"Well, good luck to them," she said as the aircraft disappeared over the mountains and the sound diminished to a distant drone. "I'd better get back to the station, Martin. See you tomorrow. Ngubane will be back soon, and maybe I can enlist him in my investigations."

"Go well, little sister," he replied. "As always, be very careful who you trust. It may be quiet right now, but I don't believe they have given up."

Back at the station, Erica switched on the computer system in the office and checked for a signal before going to her study and opening up her mail. There were two messages, one from Nick Van Heerden, her sometime boyfriend from school—son of a local farmer, he was expected to work on the farm during his holidays, so she did not see much of him. The other was from Ainu at the department head office. Nick did not have much to say—he was a boy of few words at the best of times, and just talked briefly about the crops, cattle and his dogs. Erica had the feeling his father was very strict and that Nick was afraid of him. She often wished he was allowed to come and visit her at the station where he could be free of the large, overbearing figure of his father for a short time, but it seemed that, apart from school, where he was a weekly boarder, he had very little freedom. She would reply to him later, but was burning with curiosity over Ainu's mail. Clicking it open, she began to read.

"Well, little bushwoman, who do you think I saw today? Your Mr Mufara, that's who. Came in to the office to drop off your Dad's monthly returns and reports and a proposal for a new vehicle in the coming financial year. He had a short meeting with the Director again, but the door was closed and the intercom off, so I couldn't eavesdrop. It was probably about the new vehicle."

Erica smiled and read on. "Oooh, he's good-looker that one. Maybe he will break up with his fancy town lady and I can get my manicured nails into him, what you think?" Ainu went on to say that she could not get any more information on Mufara. His file was missing from the main staff records cabinet and she could not get past the password on the computerised system.

"But, I am a determined little witch, and I'll keep digging. See ya."

Erica shut down her laptop and sat back, thinking about Mufara.

"Maybe when he comes back I should just have it out with him," she thought to herself. "More and more he is fading as my main suspect, but there is certainly something not right . . ."

The roar of the returning helicopter brought Erica out of her reverie, and she went out to watch the landing, gentle as a dragonfly, dust and leaves flying, on the concrete helipad near the water tower. Her father got out and walked to the office, while the pilot and technician started checking and refuelling the machine.

"How was it?" she asked her father as he stood in front of the big wall map, using a smaller one in his hand to mark some lines on the larger one.

"It is amazing how much ground you can cover in such a short space of time and how much you see from up there," he enthused.

"Didn't see us right under your nose," Erica thought to herself, at the same time realising that they were not even really searching during the take off phase.

"The downside," he went on, "is the noise. You can't creep up on animals or people in those things. Some old elephant cow on the other side fell down in a dead faint when we came over. I felt bad, but saw she was up and running a few seconds later."

She wondered what Martin would have to say about that as her father continued.

"It would be perfect as a follow-up once we sight poachers on the ground—they would never make it to the fence before we had them, but this pattern of flying is unlikely to turn anything up. I am sending out all the available game guards today, in small parties, to cover as much ground as possible. They will base up on high ground and just quietly observe. We will hide the helicopter at a central position and listen out for the guards on the radio 24 hours a day."

He marked the observation posts for the guards and a likely campsite for the helicopter on the main map and asked Erica, "Sorry to do this so soon after the last patrol, but I feel I must be with the helicopter team. It'll be a maximum of a week. Will you be OK here? I could use you as a relay station operator for the radio, together with Chimemwe—how do you feel about that?"

Erica replied that she would have no problem at all—she was just as determined to stop the poachers as anyone else.

"Just don't forget you promised me at least one ride in the helicopter before it goes home." She reminded her father as she headed back to her study. She owed a reply to Nick and should do it now before it slipped her mind. He really was a nice guy—painfully shy around her, but fiercely protective if he thought she was ever being bullied. They had held hands once or twice, strolling behind the blue gums at the bottom of the playing fields after prep, but she was not sure whether they were actually boy-and-girl friend yet. She liked him and thought he was honest and caring, but there was a sad side to his green-brown eyes when he thought she was not looking. He was by far the best looking boy at school, tall and lean, permanently tanned from working on the farm, with his naturally dark hair faded to gold by the sun. She tapped out a chatty mail, telling him about the poachers and the helicopter but leaving out Martin for the time being. He would think that she had got sunstroke or just gone plain potty out in the bush. She ended by repeating her previous invitations for him to come and spend some time on the reserve.

Erica glanced out of her window towards the parade-ground in front of the main office. The game guards were gathering, dumping their gear on the lawn and going to the stores to draw their rations, radios and rifles. The helicopter crew were securing extra drums of fuel to the skids and packing their gear into the aircraft. Erica's dad was preparing the Land Rover and getting his camping gear together. She went over to help him get his clothes packed into the small duffel bag, hiding a selection of Wilson's biscuits and some sweets as a surprise for him at the bottom.

"Ngubane should be back tomorrow, Erica. Mufara will collect him on his way back from town. They should be here before sundown, and I'll collect Ngubane the next day by car or helicopter if we happen to be flying at the right time. Would you show him on the big map where we are and what the plan is?" were his last words as he hugged her and strode towards the waiting vehicle with all the guards perched on top or inside.

"Sure thing, Dad. I'll let you know by radio as soon as they come in. Take care out there, OK?"

The helicopter started with its characteristic whine and then the whop, whop, whop of the blades slowly turning until they were a blur, slowly lifting off with the heavy load and setting off over the distant hills. The station was suddenly quiet, just the dust from the helicopter's downdraught settling back to the ground. Erica felt a pang of fear for her father. They should just be doing the work of taking care of the wildlife and the reserve, not fighting a battle with real guns against an unseen enemy. Shaking off her premonition she wandered over to Mufara's office, wondering if he had left his diary behind, but found the desk clear and neat, no books in sight. She checked the drawers, but only found the usual office clutter of pens, pencils, paper clips and staples.

"Oh well, I guess he needs his diary in town to list his errands. Nothing sinister in that," she muttered to herself as she left the office, closing the door behind her.

She spent the late afternoon with Martin, briefing him on the plan and describing the places where the guards and central camp would be. He decided to go out into the reserve as well, making contact with the herds and getting all the animals they communicated with to keep an eye out for poachers or strangers.

"I'll contact you as soon as we have anything, and you can get the news through to your dad, although I don't know how you are going to tell him you have a bulletin from a warthog down in sector five!" said Martin, looking steadily at her.

"Oh, I'll think of something," she said. "You be careful too—I don't want to see you hurt doing something silly. If you are in doubt, run like the wind and try and get back to the station or my dad's camp . . ."

They parted as the last glow of sunset faded against the clear sky of the west.

5. An Imposter
In Our Midst

The station grew calm and silent after the flurry of activity of the departing rangers and helicopter crew, and Erica settled down to wait for news by radio or from Martin's bush network. The gate guard had just called in to let her know that Mufara and Ngubane had signed in and would be at the station within half an hour, and she had forwarded this to her father. Dark clouds were looming in the east and the distant thunder sounded like a lion's roar, a sure sign of coming rain, probably in the late afternoon. It would bring relief from the heat and provide much-needed moisture for the dry earth, but would make the patrols' job cold and miserable at night. If it rained heavily, some streams and rivers would come down in flash floods and make crossing impossible or dangerous. At least it would make life difficult for poachers as well.

Erica went over to Wilson's kitchen domain and asked him to prepare sandwiches and tea for Ngubane and Mufara, as she assumed they had missed out on lunch, and Ngubane might need to leave shortly to join the base camp team.

She heard the sound of the pick-up truck rumbling towards the station and went over to the office to meet the returning men. They pulled up outside the office door, and Ngubane sprang out with a greeting and a hand-clasp to her shoulder, in the way of his tribe.

"Wow, you've grown since I last saw you!" he grinned at her fondly. "Ease up on Wilson's porridge or you'll turn into a Masai giant."

Erica laughed at his easy way of teasing her, and led them into the office, both of them now carrying office supplies, mail and parcels collected in the capital and Rafinga. Wilson brought them their snack, and they all sat around the office reception table while Erica brought them up to date on the events of the past few days.

"Dad may want you to join them, Ngubane, but I am waiting for him to call back with instructions—they will come up on radio schedule at five this evening—maybe you should take that call," Erica said to him.

"Sure, no problem, I'll do that," he replied. Mufara got up, thanked Erica for the meal and said he needed to offload the fresh supplies with Wilson and get back to his office to get his spares and paperwork in order.

After he had left, Erica showed Ngubane on the wall map the position of the lookout guards and the central base camp, and outlined the plan. Once done, she asked him how his leave had been.

He lightly brushed it off, saying, "Oh you know, it is difficult going back to the traditional ways after being away so long. My grandfather never went to school, and even my father cares more about his cattle than most other things. He thinks I should be there to take over the farm when he is too old, and does not understand that I can never return to that way of life. Sure, maybe when I am retired, it would be good to sit back and enjoy the simplicity and lack of stress, but somehow I don't think so . . ."

They traded bits and pieces of news for a while before Ngubane went to get settled back into his cottage and unpack, then repack for a week in the bush if he was called at short notice.

Erica went back to her study after booting up the office computer and switching on the wireless connection. There was no mail from Ainu, just a short one from Aunt Fran in England, chatting about the weather and cost of everything, and another from Nick, saying he had asked his father if he could come to the reserve for a few days, but this had been refused. Erica got the idea, reading between the lines that it had caused an argument between them. She felt a twinge of guilt that she had asked him in the first place and hoped he was not in trouble. She wondered how his father could imagine that Nick would stay on the farm when he was old enough to make his own decisions if he was treated this way as a growing boy. If it was her, she would already be making plans to get as far away as possible when the time was right. There was nothing she could do but give Nick her support, and was so grateful her own father gave her the freedom to make choices within a common-sense framework of rules. Chores had to be done, and he required certain standards of behaviour from her, but there was always time for fun, hobbies and even solitude when she needed to be alone. She enjoyed applying herself at school, apart from a couple of subjects she found boring and a waste of time, so there was no friction between them on that score. Mr van Heerden was probably not a bad man, but he must have had a hard childhood or something to be so strict with Nick. There were no other children in the family, and maybe that was part of the problem, that he saw Nick as his only link to the future, a future of his own imagination. His mother, who Erica had only met briefly once when she came to collect Nick from school, was a timid and shy woman, seldom seen in the village without her husband at her side.

"Hmm, maybe I should change my thoughts about being a biologist and become a psychologist, the way I'm analysing people at the moment," Erica thought to herself, shutting down her computer and wondering how Mufara's meetings with his girlfriend had gone.

She wandered over to his office where he had just finished packing away his spares and was bundling the packaging into the recycling bins in the workshop.

"Hello again, Erica," he said, dusting his hands off and moving back towards the office. "Tea?"

"Yes, please," replied Erica, producing a foil-wrapped pack of biscuits she had already pinched from the kitchen. "This could become habit-forming," he said with a smile, "Wilson sure bakes a mean biscuit. What are you going to say when he discovers the jar is half empty?"

"Oh, I think he will forgive me," she replied, "He is such a dear old thing . . ."

They busied themselves with the tea tray and sat down at his desk. Erica asked about the trip to the capital, not directly referring to Mufara's personal life, but he of course knew exactly what she was up to.

"I know you are dying to hear about my love life, young lady, and I'll tell you that right now it is okay. We talked it out and decided to give it another six months, by which time I will have organised a transfer or she will have come to terms with living with me on the station. I am sure now that she is not seeing anyone else, and we have agreed to be patient with each other . . ."

"Oh, it would be shame for you to leave here after only having just begun—we would miss you," Erica said with genuine regret.

"Well, as you know," he replied, "Life has a habit of changing—it is the one certain thing after death and taxes, and we have to see the change as opportunity, not adversity. I think that's how a certain young lady of my acquaintance would put it, not so?" he grinned at her.

"Okay, you got me there—I am a bit of a busybody—got it from my Aunt Fran no doubt—she always wants to know everything about everybody. But I am really glad that you have made up with your girl friend," Erica blushed a little.

"Actually, fiancé," his grin broadened. "If we make it through the next six months and things work out, we have agreed to get married in a year or so. No hurry, but the commitment is there."

Erica felt good about his apparent happiness and they chatted on easily. Mufara said he had applied for a new vehicle for the station and had given a justification in person to the Director. He thought it would be approved in the next budget year.

"Dad will get a bigger head than he has now, driving a brand new Land Rover. He will probably not let anyone else near it!" she giggled at the thought.

It was getting toward late afternoon when Erica left Mufara's office and walked over to the radio room to see if Ngubane had kept his schedule. He was sitting at the radio set, watching the clock on the wall above it.

"Hi, Erica, just waiting for the big hand and little hand to meet at the right places. Do you want to speak to your dad?"

"Not unless he wants me," she replied. "You guys have enough on your plate to worry about family chit-chat. Just tell him I'm fine. I'm going for my daily walk to the kopje. Won't be too long, see you later."

She strolled out of the gate and then trotted quickly all the way to the small hill under the darkening sky.

"Martin?" she looked around. "You there?" Silence echoed back at her. She was disappointed, but knew he was probably far away, making contact with the herds.

She started back to the station, head down and thinking, when she suddenly saw another cigarette filter lying off the side of the track. There were no new footprints, and a herd of zebra had recently passed over the track, completely obscuring any sign she might have picked up.

Pocketing the butt, she returned to the base and let Wilson know she would be in for supper whenever he called for her. She added the butt to her growing collection and wondered who could be dropping them. Ngubane came over to her house and let her know all was well with her father and the team, even though the clouds were steadily building and there was an oppressive feel to the air. One of the guards was coming back to collect him with the Land Rover early the next morning.

A few fat drops of rain eventually fell from the sky, puffing tiny craters in the dust of the parking area before breaking into a torrential downpour. The evening sun lowered beneath the storm clouds, giving an eerie texture to the falling rain, golden-red streamers of light lancing into the ground. Thunder roared and lightning flashed, and Erica shivered despite the fact that she normally loved the rainstorms whenever they came. The sun slipped below the horizon, and now the rain fell steadily, invisible in the darkness, but audible with a dozen different noises. It rattled on the tin roofs of the buildings, plashed into the now muddy ground and pattered on the leaves of trees before rushing away to swell thirsty streams and rivers.

Erica grabbed an old umbrella standing by the door and ran over to the kitchen area, getting her feet thoroughly muddy on the way. She wiped them off and entered the kitchen, meeting Wilson coming the other way, also holding an umbrella.

"I was just coming to get you, Missy Erica!" he exclaimed. "You should not be out in this weather alone . . ."

"Why, Wilson, you reckon maybe the Tokoloshe are out and about? I don't think so—they probably don't have little umbrellas."

With a sniff, Wilson returned to his stove.

"Supper will be ready in five minutes. Why don't you sit at the kitchen table—it will be wet on the veranda."

Wilson pulled out a chair and cleared a space for her at the big kitchen work table and she sat, enjoying the warmth of the old wood stove in the unusual cold. They chatted back and forth easily, as old friends do. Wilson mentioned that he should probably do some baking soon, as the biscuits seemed to be getting low. Without missing a beat, Erica replied that she had packed some for her father and the other guards, that would probably explain it. He just smiled and carried on stirring the big pot, from which delicious aromas wafted across the room.

6. Mr Bamjee's Emporium

The days sped past with no news from the bush camps or guards. Ngubane had left, the rain had tapered off during that night, but nobody had seen anything at all unusual in the reserve since then. Martin had been in touch with his long-distance rumble, also reporting that all was quiet.

"Maybe it's become too hot for them here and they have gone somewhere else to hunt," she thought to herself.

It was decided to end the operation after six fruitless days. The helicopter came in first, bringing her father along as well.

"I thought I'd enjoy a last ride before we lose this magnificent flying machine," he said to her as he stepped out, ducking below the slowing rotors. "I have organised for you to be given a ride to Rafinga in the chopper. They pass right overhead and can drop you on the soccer field. I'll send Mufara in to collect you and do the mail and supply run."

Erica trotted off to change her clothes, excited at the prospect of the flight. She remembered to take her small digital camera and notebook, slipping them into her pocket on the way out. The helicopter team had unloaded the machine and refuelled, packing their own bags neatly under the rear seats. The pilot invited Erica to sit in the front left seat where the engineer normally sat, and after she was strapped in, he flicked a bank of switches and the rotors started slowly turning as the scream of the engine rose. Even through the intercom headset the pilot had given her, the sound penetrated her body, slowly easing out into a steady roar. The blades turned into a silver disc and then there was a change in their beat as the machine lifted off, nose slightly down. The station seemed to shrink as they rose above the trees and turned south for Rafinga. The pilot kept the altitude low enough so Erica could see any wildlife, but not so low as to scare the more timid. The zebra just wheeled about a bit, kicking up dust, taking the opportunity to nip and kick each other in the confusion. The wildebeest of course went totally crazy, legs akimbo, running around in small circles with the whites of their eyes showing, but they do this at least twenty times a day, often for no reason at all. The giraffe ran a few ungainly paces on their stilt-like legs before resuming their dainty browsing off the tops of the acacia trees. A herd of impala flowed like pale water over a cataract as they crested a low rise. Suddenly the pilot wheeled the helicopter around in a tight circle, crushing Erica into her seat. His trained eyes had found something.

"Look down there, Erica!" he spoke excitedly through the headset, pointing to a small thicket of bush near three isolated palm trees.

She strained at first to see what he was talking about, when suddenly a pride of lion sprang into focus. Almost perfectly camouflaged by the pale grass and shadow, they lay with ears flattened and tails twitching at this intrusion on their most important pastime—sleeping. Erica took a few shots with her camera, knowing they would not be great without a telephoto lens, but good enough for her father or Ngubane to recognise the individuals from the lion data book. She pencilled their location in her notebook, and grinned broadly at the pilot, giving him a thumbs-up.

"A pleasure, my dear, but now we must fly. Time really is money with this little baby."

They gained altitude and crossed the reserve boundary fence a few minutes later. Following the main road to Rafinga, the odd car looked like a crawling beetle, and it seemed like seconds before they were landing gently on the rather patchy town soccer field. With a quick goodbye from both men, they took off immediately and headed off into the south, the sound quickly diminishing. A small crowd of children and quite a few adults had gathered at the field, wondering who was important enough to be dropped off, and hoping for a closer look at the exotic machine. Many of them knew Erica, and greeted her in some awe as she nonchalantly strolled across the field to the rusty old gate.

"I think I shall have one of those when I am grown up," Erica smiled to herself. "Such a civilised way of travel, my deah."

Erica walked into the village and made her way to Aunt's house, her heart still pounding from the excitement of the flight. She always had her own key, and had promised to check up now and then. The house was still and quiet, but very clean. Aunt Fran's housekeeper had been coming in every few days to water the plants and garden and dust the house down, and everything was in order. She went to the post office to clear out Aunt Fran's box, which was just about bursting, mostly with junk and magazines. She took it all back to the house and sorted it into piles on the hall table, not seeing anything that looked urgent. A hoot from the driveway announced Mufara's arrival.

"Hi, Erica. I have some errands to run, want to come with me, or do you have stuff to do here?" he asked.

"I need a few minutes," she replied, "I have already picked up the station mail, so don't worry about the post office. Why don't you meet me at the café for a snack before we leave, say eleven-thirty?"

"Sounds good to me. See you there," he replied, backing out into the street and heading for the government depot.

Erica finished tidying up, collected a book she wanted from her bedroom at the back of the house and locked up. She wandered back into the village, window shopping and picking up a few things here and there. As she passed one of the side streets, she saw a man emerge from one of the shanty-style shops that had grown up over the years. He was wearing dark glasses and 'town' clothes, not the sort of shirt that many people wore out here, and the two-tone shoes were a dead give-away. A cigarette dangled from his lips, and he appeared to be staring right at her, but it was impossible to tell with the sun reflecting off the tinted wrap-around 'shades'. She walked on, wondering why he had caught her eye, apart from standing out a bit.

She went right around the block, coming back to the side street from the other end. She saw the store the man had come out of was 'M Bamjee's Emporium. Hardware, Haberdashery, Fine Tailors and General Goods'. He was just turning onto the main street, and she saw him toss his cigarette carelessly onto the sidewalk.

"Pig," she thought to herself. Apart from the litter, in this part of Africa you never threw a lit cigarette anywhere. Bushfires could be devastating to animals and humans alike.

She hurried after him, with half a mind to tell him off about his habits, but slowed down as she reached the place where he had tossed the butt. Even as she bent down to look, she knew it was the same brand as the ones she had in her study. She pretended to be tying her shoelace as she quickly stubbed it out and slipped it into her hand. She did not like the smell or feel of the still hot filter, but closed her fingers around it. She found a handkerchief in her pocket and wrapped the butt in it, slipping it back into her pocket. She looked around but nobody seemed to be watching, so she carried on following her new suspect.

He made a left turn at the next street, the same one Erica had used to go around the back way, and it seemed they were now embarked on a merry-go-round of Rafinga. When she got to the corner, he was gone.

"Eh?" she remarked to herself. He couldn't have just disappeared.

She hurried on, peering into each of the three small shops on this street, but he was not in any of them. At the next corner, he was still missing, and all the buildings in this road were the back ends of the bigger stores of the main road, with 'no entry' signs and gates, or guarded storage yards. A security guard at one of the gates recognised Erica and asked if she needed help, having seen her go round the block twice.

"Did you see a man go past here?" she asked. "He was dressed like a townie with fancy dark glasses."

"Yes, miss, I saw him walk fast past here and wondered what his hurry was."

She thanked him and walked on, retracing her steps around to Mr Bamjee's Emporium. She entered the slightly darkened interior, taking a few seconds for her eyes to recover from the glare of daylight. Her first sensation was the not unpleasant mingled smells of spices, raw and cooked nuts, dried fish, new calico cloth and many others not immediately identifiable. As her sight returned, she saw that a counter ran the whole width of the back of the store, and the walls were covered top to bottom with shelves, groaning under the weight of every type of ware known to civilisation. Hanging from the rafters were hangers with children's dresses and shirts, watering cans and axe heads, interspersed with fly papers well endowed with flies. The floor space was shared, or rather fought over, by opened sacks of beans, rice, sugar and maize meal. A doorway to the left of the counter was half concealed by a curtain of old bottle tops threaded on string. A transistor radio ('Special Offer, only $99.99') blared out tinny eastern music and 'Mike' running shoes (the 'M' cunningly designed to look like an 'N') were also on sale at, yes, $99.99. Or easy payments of $10 per week until (period unreadable). Her three hundred and sixty degree survey ended up back at the counter, where a wizened little man dressed in a long white dishdasha watched her with hooded eyes framing his sharp nose.

She immediately thought 'Golum' from the Lord of the Rings and then decided she was being unfair.

"Good morning, young miss," the nut-brown gnome seemed to hiss as he wrung his hands together. "What can my poor establishment do for you on this very fine day?"

Erica was a bit taken aback and renewed her Golum thoughts, but soon recovered and said, "Oh, I'm just looking around, thanks. You certainly have a lot of stuff in here!"

"And if I don't have it, I'll get it. My very motto and promise," was his quick reply. "Just let me know if I can help you," he continued, returning to the large ledger on the counter where he was making notes.

Erica browsed for a while, selecting some notepads which she saw were cheaper than the same brand at the supermarket.

"Do you perhaps have a toilet?" she asked as she placed the notebooks on the counter, gesturing towards the door.

"No, no, sorry young miss, that is private. The café on the main street will let you use their very fine facilities . . ."

Erica backed down and paid for her purchases, and then asked, "I'm looking for a gift for someone. Something a little different. Do you have any jewellery, say a bangle in ivory or elephant hair?"

The man looked directly into her eyes and said in a perfectly even voice, no hiss, no sibilant whisper, "Miss Granger, do not play games with me. I am probably a hundred years older than you in every way you can imagine. I know as you do that trade in ivory is banned in this country. I am an honest businessman and I know the law. I also know your father, regretfully not under the best circumstances. That will be $3.50 for the note pads, I have given you a 10% discount, have a very good day . . ."

Erica's face burned as she left the shop clutching a paper bag in one hand. She had a glance down the alley that led down the side of the store, littered with cartons, tins and an old washing machine. She could see that the side door led onto the alley, and the end of the alley appeared to be the living quarters of the shop, a neat door flanked by flower boxes with splashes of colour relieving the dinginess of the alley. To one side of the door a small window looked out, and she thought she saw the curtain twitch slightly before she turned away.

Erica made her way to the café, greeted the owner and ordered a milkshake. She went to the toilet and thoroughly washed her hands of the smell of the cigarette. She rolled the butt up in toilet paper and threw her handkerchief in the rubbish bin. She was a bit early for Mufara and went to the magazine rack to select a few old editions to page through while waiting. She kept one eye on the main street outside, hoping for another glimpse of the Smoking Man, but he did not show.

"Probably a totally innocent insurance salesman from the city, doing a country tour . . ." she thought to herself, again berating herself for being the dumbest detective this side of Get Smart. "Good one back there at the store, trying to trap the storekeeper into an ivory deal. Clever me."

Mufara eventually arrived, and they had a toasted sandwich each before setting off back to the reserve, an uneventful trip interspersed with idle chat above the noise of the truck engine.

"I hear the patrols had no luck out in the bush," he remarked.

"Yes, my dad said it was even quieter than usual. No villagers taking shortcuts across the eastern corner, no snares found on the trails, no spoor, nothing," she replied. "It seems we are off the poaching menu, for a while anyway."

They arrived home well before dark and Erica joined her father in his office as he was tidying up the end of his day. She dropped the mail on the reception desk and brought across the two-day old newspaper she had found for him. After telling him about the wonderful helicopter ride and lion sighting, she asked him about Mr Bamjee, and he looked up suddenly.

"What is that old rascal up to now? What's he got to do with you?"

She described how she innocently went into his store and bought some books and how, in conversation it came about that they knew each other.

"Know each other?" he snorted. "I'll say we know each other. The last time I saw that venerable gentleman he was in court being defended by one of the best lawyers in the country against charges of dealing in leopard skins, charges brought by yours truly."

"What happened?" asked Erica, dreading the reply that maybe he had spent a hundred years behind bars and was now seeking revenge.

"Oh, as usual, a slap on the wrist fine and an admonishment not to deal in animal trophies of any description for ten years," he said. "But, the old pirate is still angry with me and we don't greet each other in the street. I don't trust him and he does not like me. Quite fine by me . . ."

When in bed that night, reading the latest Harry Potter (for the second time) Erica heard Martin calling her. She got up and walked to her window, opening it to get a clearer link to him. "I've just got back from the other side of the park," he pushed his thoughts towards her as clear as if he was in the room. "I'm close by now, in the Mopane forest, you know, keeping an eye on things . . ."

"And having a bit of a leaf fest no doubt, hmm?" she projected back at him.

"Sorry, you're breaking up a bit there. Hello operator, operator . . ." Martin made strange clicking noises and Erica had to chuckle out loud, hoping nobody could see or hear her at her window, laughing at the night sky.

"I'll see you tomorrow, same place, same time?" he asked. "Have a good night little Sister . . ."

"Good night, Brother, have a good . . . do you sleep? I never asked. I have never seen an elephant lying down, tucked up under a duvet of leaves. How do you manage?"

"Well, we doze a lot, not that we are a dozy lot, you understand. Some of us do actually lie down, but only when we are absolutely sure it is safe, and not all of us lie down at the same time. I tend to sleep on my feet or leaning against a big tree with my tusks tips on the ground," he explained.

"Well, have a good stand, or doze or lean, see you tomorrow," Erica raised a hand to the stars in farewell and went back to the world of Hogwarts, where the magic seemed no less real than her own life.

7. ELEPHANT GRAVEYARD

After a quick breakfast with her father and Ngubane, where the discussion centred around the failure of the patrols and helicopter to find any trace of poachers, Erica packed a shoulder bag and set off for her meeting with Martin. Once again, the feeling was that the poachers knew exactly what was going on in the reserve and had stayed well away during the operation. She thought about it as she walked, wondering if all her suspicions were so far off the mark as to be laughable. She was so deeply engrossed in her thoughts that she almost walked into Martin, standing quietly on the track waiting for her.

"Whoa!" he exclaimed, "Watch where you are going little lady. I may have been a hungry lion just sitting here with my mouth open waiting for you to stroll in. Yummy. Just a morsel, but yummy nonetheless."

Erica shared her thoughts with him, telling him about the trip to Rafinga and the mysterious Smoking Man, Mr Bamjee and her foul-up there.

"I have a feeling you are starting to push some buttons, Erica. You must be careful now. If they are involved and suspect you may be onto something, they can be ruthless. There is too much money at stake for them to turn away from this business," he said with a worried tone.

"I don't think they see me as a threat, just a silly girl asking silly questions," she replied as they walked towards the kopje.

"Come on up, I want to show you something," said Martin, changing the subject.

Erica nimbly mounted up and settled behind Martin's head and he walked at a steady but rapid pace towards the mountains.

"How much time do you have?" he asked as the valleys and ravines of the massive flat-topped plateau grew closer.

"Oh, no problem, I told my dad I'd be away for the morning, and I've brought a small handset radio along so I can call him if I need to," she replied.

Martin headed for what seemed to be a blind ravine, choked with stunted trees and dense bush mixed in with tumbled boulders the size of houses. Pushing aside the bush, he forced his bulk through a narrow cleft, his ears pushing against Erica's thighs.

"Okay up there?" he asked.

"No problem, your ears are great as leather cowboy chaps!" she said as she ducked under a low-lying branch.

Looking back, Erica could see no sign of the entrance they had come through and realised that it could take an army a lifetime to find their way into this narrow defile. The walls either side of them were sheer rock, and the rock-strewn path smoothed out until it was a sandy river bed. The ravine twisted and turned, sometimes almost doubling back on itself. It was so deep that the sun only touched the river bed in odd places with a dappled light filtering through the bushes high up on the edges, and it was cool and quiet.

"What a beautiful place!" Erica exclaimed. "It almost feels like a church."

"Funny you should say that," Martin said quietly, but nothing more, as he plodded on. They continued in companionable silence for another fifteen minutes, until suddenly the narrow walls fell away and they entered an amphitheatre of rock surrounding a small plain, densely wooded with spreading acacia trees. Erica could see odd shapes scattered around, white against the green of the grass, like dead bleached trees and rocks. Martin said nothing, but walked slowly forward, approaching the nearest tumbled pile.

"It's a skeleton!" Erica exclaimed, recognising now the ribs, spine, skull and massive leg bones of an elephant. "And the tusks!" She could hardly believe the size of the creamy-coloured arcs of pure ivory lying near the massive guano-streaked skull.

"Yes, that was my paternal grandfather—a wise old man who lived out his years in peace." Martin picked up one of the smaller bones in the tip of his trunk and brought it to his mouth, inhaling the scent.

"What is this place?" Erica whispered in awe.

"You have probably heard of the myths of the elephant graveyards of Africa," Martin replied quietly. "Well, this is ours. Long before there were white men or even black men, when only the little yellow people coexisted with us, long before fences and guns and cars and 'planes, this was our place to come and die in peace. When a member of the herd knows he or she is no longer able to keep up and the teeth can no longer crush the leaves and bark, when the eyesight is fading and the bones aching, this is our final refuge."

He carefully replaced the bone and walked around the plain, showing Erica dozens of skeletons, most of them complete with tusks, some worn and broken, but a king's ransom just lying on the ground.

"My God, if the poachers knew about this, they would do anything to get in here," she said, almost looking over her shoulder to spot imaginary invaders. "How come nobody has found this place before? With aerial surveys and choppers flying about the reserve it seems impossible it has not been spotted."

"I think that from the air this small bowl is very hard to define," he went on, "The thick trees certainly help hide the skeletons and the shadows thrown by the high rim make it hard to get a good picture of what is below. As you saw, the entrance is secret and difficult to get through, but most of all, we trust in the spirits of our ancestors to draw a veil across this place when strangers are near. Our collective and ancient thoughts gently turn away a questing eye without the seeker even knowing he has been diverted."

"And yet you brought me here, one of the species engaged in your destruction," Erica whispered.

"I have no secrets from you, little one. And this is my measure of trust in you. You cannot tell anyone, even your father of this place. Perhaps your grandchildren may earn the right . . ."

They stood in silence under the canopy of a giant thorn tree, and Erica felt a sense of absolute peace descend upon her.

Looking at the gnarled trunk of the acacia, amongst the whorls and twists of bark, she suddenly saw her mother's face, perfect in every detail. Her voice seeming to come from within Erica's mind, "I'm proud of you, my daughter. You are going to do good things in your life. I will love you always."

The vision faded away and Erica bent forward until her forehead touched the back of Martin's head and her tears fell upon him like summer rain. Martin reached back over his shoulder with his trunk and gently stroked her hair.

"Yes, I also heard—she has earned her place in this place of peace. She is happy where she is, don't grieve for her."

Erica sat up, smiled, and held onto his trunk as he turned away towards the ravine. They walked on like that, trunk in hand, or hand in trunk, until they reached the hidden entrance. Martin paused and listened for a long while before pushing through the tangled bush, turning to rearrange branches that had been moved. He plucked a leafy branch from a tree some distance away and holding it in his trunk, swept away the tracks they had made.

Time had flown and it was almost midday when Erica made a call on the handset, but there was no reception.

"Funny," she said, "These mobiles can reach over sixty miles, and it's a straight line back to the station."

"Just wait a few minutes," Martin advised her. "I think our ancestors' power of diversion may extend to modern technology . . ."

Erica did not want to argue with that bit of nonsense, but waited until they were a short distance from the base of the mountains. The reception bar suddenly popped up in the window of the handset and she called the station, getting an immediate response from Chimemwe who said she would let her father know she was fine and on the way home. Martin dropped her off at their usual meeting place and they parted reluctantly.

"I guess it's now a game of wait and see," he said. "But stay alert, don't get into trouble."

"The same goes for you, Brother Elephant. Take care."

8. SCAR

The group of fifteen men moved furtively through the bush. Using only hand signs learned both in the military and their upbringing in a hunter's environment, they had almost a sixth sense of what their lead scout was seeing and telling them.

Only six of the men carried rifles, high-powered Draganov sniping rifles previously property of the Zambesian Army, lost in transit. The remainder of the party carried the tools of their bloody trade—machetes, short-handled axes, skinning knives, transport slings, rope and burlap sacking.

All were dressed in nondescript brown and green fatigues, overalls and cast-off camouflage jackets. All wore the same type of boot, also army issue, hard wearing canvas uppers with thick rubber soles, ideal for bush conditions. No shining objects could be seen. No rings, bangles, necklaces or watches. All potential reflective surfaces had been dulled with a mixture of soot and goat fat, and any loose equipment had long since been tied down securely to prevent the slightest click or tinkle of sound.

For some of the older members of the raiding party, it brought back memories of the long bush war, where the retaliation and consequences were swift for lapses in concentration and training. For the younger, it was an adventure with good rewards, and they felt invulnerable in their stealth and the knowledge that they were being looked after by higher powers on the outside.

They had crossed the fence into the reserve after sundown, using a thickly wooded and rocky section where their movements would be difficult to detect. The vehicle party had dropped them off a few miles from the crossing point and would wait for them for as long as it took. The leader of the poachers carried a satellite phone duplicated by the one held by the senior driver, and he would know when and where to move into position for a rapid uplift of men and trophies. Several different vehicles would share the loads and disperse in various directions, making a concerted follow-up difficult for the Police or Wildlife authorities.

As the dusk deepened into the true darkness of Africa, with a swath of brilliant stars and a slice of sickle moon, the men slowed their pace, reliant on the head tracker and his two outriders, now using night-vision goggles, also courtesy of the national army central armoury.

They had cut across the tracks of a large breeding herd of elephant soon after crossing into the park, but the spoor was several hours old, and they would be hard pressed to catch up in a direct competition of speed and stamina.

The head tracker knew the reserve intimately and also knew well the habits of a herd on the move, slowed by the youngsters and needing frequent stops for foraging and water. He estimated a course across country that would save them miles and put them in a position to be upwind and in an ambush position. Discussing his strategy with the leader of the band and getting approval, he diverted off the spoor and led the men towards a low range of hills, avoided by the elephant because of the razor-sharp dolomite ripples in the rock, standing up like icing on a surrealistic cake. The men's army boots would protect them for as long as the rubber lasted, but woe betide any human or animal cast adrift in this little ocean of unforgiving stone.

The leader of the gang called a halt once they had entered the range of hills and were almost on the crest. He signalled for an hour's break and the porters set about making tea on small gas burners and breaking out dried meat and cold cooked maize porridge into equal portions for all. The hunters moved automatically into a defensive perimeter, covering all approaches to the lying up point and had their rations delivered to them by the porters.

The leader of the group, a short but heavily-muscled man with a jagged scar running from temple to chin across the corner of his right eye and two fingers missing from his left hand, took out several items from his pack. Switching on a small GPS receiver, he unfolded a survey map of the reserve and pinpointed their position, making some notes in the margin of the map. Firing up the satellite phone, he muttered a few words to the person who answered and then shut everything down, taking a mouthful of tea and some cold porridge, bland and distasteful as it was.

He leant back against a commiphora tree, the papery peeling bark rustling softly, and closed his eyes, reflecting on the circumstances that had brought him to this place. Poaching was not his profession or preference, but as a wanted man across three countries, he was running out of options and places of refuge. Once a highly decorated veteran of the vicious bush war to the east, he had been sidelined after the "victory" and like many of his comrades was virtually forced into a life of crime to survive.

His dreams of retiring to a small family farm in the foothills of the Chimanimani Mountains were dashed after his first ambush on a security van carrying wages to an army base, where he was recognised by one of the armed guards, an ex-soldier from his previous unit. A series of armed robberies across the country followed and were correctly or incorrectly attributed to him and his growing gang of professional thieves. When the pressure became too intense, they crossed into the neighbouring states, making contact with old friends and setting up similar raids.

Eventually caught in an ambush after an informer pinpointed the next raid, he was lucky to escape with his life, crawling into the bush with terrible injuries to his face and hand. Slipping into a nearby river and floating away from the search party, he managed to haul himself out some miles downstream, only to find himself looking into the barrel of a pistol held in the rock-steady hand of a tall man in army uniform with reflective dark glasses.

"Oh well, it was good while it lasted," he grimaced up through the blood still seeping across his face, "Go ahead and do it, no point in going through the farce of a trial, is there?"

"Not so fast, friend," replied the man, squatting now and examining the wounds. "Looks bad, but I think they are just flesh wounds. The fingers, or lack of, need stitching for sure, but I think you'll make it."

What followed was almost a dream. The loss of blood had made him weak and dizzy, but he remembered being led to a vehicle, a few hours on bad roads, a visit to a clinic at a missionary station somewhere and then the camp hidden deep in the bush near the northern border.

"Rest, recover and recuperate," said his saviour before leaving him in the care of a mixed bunch of ruffians from every corner of the sub-continent. "We'll speak soon."

He was soon fully recovered and ready within a few weeks to go on the run again, but before he could make a move, the army officer was back and called him to the shade of a large tree for a meeting. They sat on upturned oil drums and the officer introduced himself as a major in the national army who had other business interests.

"Listen, Scar, I have a proposal for you. I have been following your career across the region and am suitably impressed," said the major. "Are you interested?"

"Do I have a choice, and what's the Scar business?" he asked.

"You have every choice. You can walk away from here now, and we will never speak again, but I am sure that the next time I see you, it will be in a coffin," the major grinned. "And, as for Scar—that is your new name, and really fitting. That's quite a gash you have there," pointing to the angry red weal snaking down the other man's face.

That meeting signalled a relationship that had lasted over five years, with the major setting up crimes that were almost impossible to trace and Scar carrying out the operations, fading back into the bush after every raid on a bank, truck or game reserve. The major muddied the waters wherever he could, and with his contacts deep inside the police and even government ministries, kept Scar and his gang always one step ahead of the law.

But, Scar was tired now. Tired of a life of constant furtive movement, looking over the shoulder and waiting for the snap of a bullet from nowhere. Tired of the companionship of vicious and stupid men who had to be kept in rein with harsh discipline. Tired of sleeping like an animal in the bush, unable to contact his wife and children for fear of endangering them. Tired.

Forcing himself up to his feet and shouldering his pack was the signal for the gang to do likewise and move on. They resumed their march, stopping every few hours for a short break before the dawn light tinted the eastern sky in hues of salmon and pink.

They had traversed the low dolomite mountain range and now looked out across a vast plain, dotted with stands of Mopani forest and occasional clumps of tall palm trees, probably indicating water nearby.

Calling his lead tracker over, Scar hunched down with his shooting team and they discussed the strategy of the next few hours. Using a twig to draw in a sandy patch, the tracker indicated the dolomite range, the main waterhole where the elephants invariably spent at least a day, the known trail they were on, and their own position.

Every one of them immediately understood where they were in relation to everything else and what must follow. The tracker pointed with his twig out across the plain and estimated that they would be in position at the waterhole by midday if they force marched, and should beat the herd which had had to take a wide loop around the mountains.

Scar immediately gave the order to move out, but not before checking each man individually, ensuring their feet were in good order, that the water bottles had been filled at the last stream and that all equipment was present and accounted for. His gang may have been brigands, but they were disciplined and motivated brigands, following a natural leader.

They arrived at the waterhole, as the lead tracker had said, before midday. There was no sign of elephant, but plenty of other game started and scampered away when they sensed the approaching human presence.

Scar deployed his shooting team in the best positions for effective fire and moved the porters well back into a copse of trees well upwind of the waterhole. Absolute silence was imposed and observed by every member, and only careful hand signs permitted communication.

The lead tracker had cut back towards the probable inbound approach of the herd and climbed a tall tree, shading his eyes with one hand and hanging on with the other. As the afternoon wore on and the tracker wondered whether he had made an error in his tactics, he suddenly saw movement less than a mile off: flash of grey against the green of the Mopani.

A hazy cloud of dust and crackling as a branch was ripped down for the younger calves to sample. Scrambling down out of his tree, cramped and sore, he trotted back to Scar's position.

"They come!" was all he had to whisper.

Scar gripped his wrist in thanks and indicated that the tracker should lie down beside and slightly back from his own position, to avoid the muzzle flash and ejected casings when the moment came. How many times had he done this, with humans as the prey? At least they could shoot back. He often felt bad about the slaughter of elephants and sometimes rhinoceros, but had little choice but to dance to the major's tune.

The herd appeared, as they often do, with no fanfare, and very little noise. Fanning out to share the waterfront with no jostling, just the normal good manners displayed by most except the babies, who ducked between mothers' legs to get to the cool mud and refreshing water. The matriarch held back, sniffing the wind for danger and looking to the three bull elephants who hung slightly back from the breeding herd. They had shown no indication of danger, but the matriarch was uneasy and would move the herd on as soon as all had drunk and sprayed themselves with water and mud to ease the annoying insect bites.

Scar pulled the stock of the rifle tightly into his shoulder and levelled the sights on the largest of the three bulls. They were after ivory, and his instructions to his team were to shoot for ivory, not size or sex of the animal. Biggest tusks first, then move down to the smaller before the herd mills away in panic.

Their weapons were not ideal for shooting elephant, where a powerful, heavy single bullet could do the job quickly. But weapons like that were expensive, rare and easy to trace. Ammunition was controlled and expensive. Their military issue weapons however had the overwhelming advantage of firepower. Even an idiot could kill an elephant at this range with an automatic rifle. Bullets were available everywhere and cost next to nothing, or could be stolen easily from lax army bases.

Moving his fire selector to single shot, Scar eased down on the trigger, crosshairs of the telescopic sight centred on the bull's chest. No point going for the brain—the rounds were likely to bounce off or cause little damage. He forbade his hunters to use automatic settings, knowing they would fire off a whole magazine in seconds, the barrel rising with the recoil and missing most of the chosen targets. Far better to 'double tap' in rapid succession, sighting again after every second shot and then pulling off another two rounds.

When it came, the sounds of his own shots were shocking in their destruction of the quiet of the bush and the peaceful behaviour of the elephants. His bull staggered backwards, and then again after round after round slammed into him.

The other shooters had waited for Scar's first shot and now poured fire into the herd, which took fatal seconds to react and start wheeling away. Some of the younger calves did not even know there was danger in the first fusillade, having never been shot at before.

It was like a scene from hell: elephants hitting the ground with loud thumps, cows screaming in rage and calves in fear, the wounded groaning in agony.

When the survivors had fled, bodies dotted the dusty plain in front of the waterhole, some still moving in spasmodic jerks. Scar and his shooting team moved amongst them, placing muzzles for the final brain shot before the butchering team came out. With terrible efficiency, the tusks were hacked out with short-handled axes, lashed to carrying poles ready for transport, empty cartridge cases were gathered up and counted against the used and full magazines and they prepared to leave.

The whole action had taken no more than an hour, but Scar knew the sound of gunfire would not go unnoticed, even in this remote place, and he urged his men on into a trot, retracing their steps back to the fence and safety. He knew that the major had an inside line to movements of scouts and patrols in the reserve, but he trusted no one and based his survival on training and instinct, only breathing freely once back in their base.

He looked back at the gathering specks in the fading sky—the vultures would imagine paradise had come early this bloody day.

9. Smoking Man

Erica woke to the sounds of raised voices and the revving of engines. She knew instantly something was wrong and quickly dressed, running across in the grey light of pre-dawn to the office where all the lights were on. Her father was standing on the steps, issuing instructions to the gathered guards. Ngubane stood by his side, marking off check lists on a clip board.

"What's happening, Dad?" she asked as she approached.

"A villager from Chapoto has just arrived, been running all night through the reserve—I cannot imagine how he found the courage," he said, indicating an exhausted young man sitting on the steps, a large cup of tea clasped in his hands and a striped blanket around his shoulders. "They heard gunfire at last light in the north-western part of the reserve."

"Oh no!" Erica cried out. "Martin!"

"What?" her father replied, "What are you talking about, Erica?"

She regained her composure and said, "Nothing, nothing—I am still half asleep. What are you going to do?"

"First things first," he replied. "We need to get this young man back home and speak to the villagers, try and get a bearing on the direction they heard the shots from, and then go in with all the force we have to investigate."

All the station vehicles were now parked in front of the office and the guards were throwing their kit on board.

"Sorry, Pumpkin, I'm off again, I'll let you know as soon as we have any news," Granger strode down to his Land Rover, checked that that the others were ready, and they streamed out of the gate in a cloud of dust and growling engines.

Erica stood with her hand half-raised in farewell, wishing upon her best star that her dad would be safe, and that Martin, dear Martin was also far away from whatever was happening.

It was midday before the VHF radio crackled to life and Chimemwe called Erica across to hear.

"I'm afraid it is the worst news, Erica," her father's voice was sombre. "The bastards have killed four elephant from the northern herd, tusks cut out and gone, tracks clear to the fence, a big hole cut and vehicle tracks on the other side, we lost them when they merged with the main road from Chapoto's turn-off."

He went on to tell her that he had called the police who said they would come and take plaster casts of the tyre tracks, but that it was too late to set up road blocks. The poachers could be anywhere within a three hundred mile radius by then.

Erica sobbed as she returned the handset to the clip. Chimemwe put her ample arms around her and said, "You cannot cry for all of Africa, but it is okay to cry for a bit at a time . . ."

Erica hugged her and let the tears flow. When she had recovered, she ran as fast as she could to her hill, scrambling to the top, scraping her knee at one point as she slipped. Her breath was caught in the back of her throat as she stood on the topmost rock and screamed both with her mind and voice, "Martin, Martin! Are you there? Please, please be there . . ."

She waited for a few seconds then faced in the opposite direction and called again, and again, covering all the points of the compass. As she was about to give up in despair, she heard him faintly on the light breeze coming from the north.

"I'm here, Erica. They have killed four of us and one of the young bulls is wounded. I am with him right now, helping him to get deeper into the forest."

Erica shuddered in relief at Martin's voice and sorrow for the wounded bull.

"I will come and see you when the rest of the herd catch up with me and can watch over my companion," he continued, his voice fading away like a whisper of leaves ruffled in the strengthening wind.

Erica walked slowly back toward the station, thinking no doubt the same thoughts her father was: the poachers had timed it perfectly, waiting for the helicopter and patrol operation to end and for all staff to be back in the base, winding down after a difficult week in the bush. They must have received precise information from someone. Lost in her thoughts, Erica did not see the person who stepped out of the bush onto the track until she was almost upon him. Her first reaction was one of fright, and she almost cried out as she looked up at the tall man, dressed in a tiger-stripe camouflage uniform, his eyes hidden by the reflective sunglasses she recognised immediately as the Smoking Man's. As if to dispel any doubts about his identity, he slowly took a last draw on the cigarette in his mouth before grinding it into the sand. She became aware of other figures on either side of the track, crouching down, almost invisible in faded uniforms and cloth caps. She caught a glimpse of light off the barrel of an automatic rifle. Erica started to relax, thinking that the Army had come to help tracking the poachers. But what were they doing here? The incident had taken place on the other side of the reserve, many miles from here. Before she could form the question, trying to clear her dry mouth, the Smoking Man spoke first.

"So, Miss Granger, quite the detective, hmm?" His voice was deep and gravelly, but any facial expressions were effectively hidden behind the impenetrable glasses. "Your interfering in things that do not concern you could be considered hazardous to your health. Something like the warnings on my cigarette packets. Cigarettes that you seem to be rather interested in."

Erica was confused but starting to get both scared and angry.

"What do you mean? Who are you? What are you doing here," she blurted, noticing the pistol showing in the canvas holster strapped to his waist, balanced on the other side by a sheathed bayonet. She now realised that he carried no badges of rank, name tag or numbers on his uniform, which was definitely ZNA or Zambesia National Army. She could see the less-faded patches where the tags fitted on with pop studs, but the tags themselves were missing.

"Ah, so many questions, so little time. Let's just say that I have some business interests in this area and you are, shall we put it, an unwelcome competitor . . ." His lips jerked upward momentarily in what may have passed for a smile, but reminded Erica more of images of feeding sharks on National Geographic.

"Right, well, I'll just be getting off home now," she said, sidestepping around the man and making off down the track again. She had gone no more than a few paces when the Smoking Man whipped around and effortlessly grabbed her by the hair, jerking her to a halt and spinning her around. She was too shocked to cry, or even speak, but tears spurted from her eyes with the sudden and vicious pain.

"Not so fast, my little one. We have business to transact, you and I," once again the quirk of lips, but the remainder of his face was stone. He spoke rapidly to the men, four of them she now saw, closing in on them. They also had the badges removed from their uniforms, except for two of them who had a parachute logo above the left hand pocket of their shirts, marking them as elite paratroopers.

"Take her," he said to one the soldiers, pushing her roughly towards him. The soldier expertly tied her hands in front of her with a plastic cable tie and then shook out a grubby cloth taken from his pack. He twisted the cloth into a bandanna and tied it tightly around her eyes.

"No talking," she heard the Smoking Man say to her. "Otherwise the next cloth goes in your mouth. We are going to walk for a few hours, a walk in the park as it were. Behave yourself and you will be alright."

Erica could do nothing but obey, stumbling along, steadied by the soldier's hand on her elbow. It seemed like an eternity before they slowed down and she heard the men whispering amongst themselves. Suddenly she heard the sound of a passing car and knew they were at the reserve boundary near the main road to Rafinga. There were no other paved roads in the area and she knew the sound of tyres on tarmac. As soon as the sound faded, they moved rapidly to the fence and she heard the sounds of wire snapping and tools being used. She was shoved through a hole in the fence, snagging her shirt as she went through. Within a few steps they stopped and she heard the sounds of car doors opening and slamming, and then the rough growl of a diesel engine pulling away. She reached up to remove the blind, only to have her hand smacked down.

"Not so fast. You thought we had left you here, but sorry to disillusion you. That was only my men taking off. We have a far better standard of transport, or at least I do," he chuckled.

She heard the sound of more doors opening, realising as he picked her up and tossed her in, that one of the doors was actually the boot lid of a car. She landed heavily, hitting her elbow on something hard, gasping in pain as the lid was slammed down. She now reached up and took off the blind, finding herself in utter darkness for a few seconds before she saw some faint lines of light at the back of the boot. The car started to move, and she heard the spray of gravel before it moved onto the paved road and accelerated away. Erica fumbled with the lock mechanism of the boot, but could find no way to trigger the release. She gave up for a few minutes, sobbing uncontrollably and wishing her Dad was here to save her. She knew it would be hours or even the next day before he knew she was missing. Wilson would know something was wrong, but unless the patrols came up on radio during the night, he would only be back at the station in the middle of the next morning.

Pulling herself together and realising she was on her own, at least for the time being, Erica started to consider her options. She could find nothing in the boot except a jack, which had no sharp edges to saw at the cable tie, and she could not get her teeth deep enough into the plastic to gnaw at it. She tried making contact with Martin, but the distance was increasing and the metal confines of the car must be affecting the transmission. She heard nothing and decided to conserve her energy, but keep thinking all the time. She had to be ready to escape when the opportunity arose, not curl up and cry like the baby they would assume her to be.

The vehicle slowed and some turns rolled Erica from side to side, and she thought they had reached Rafinga, recognising the two bends that slowed traffic coming into the village. She was right, as they now came to a halt for the only stop-street in town, the gears changing down and then up as he drove on. A few more turns she did not recognise and the car stopped, reversed for some distance and stopped again, the engine dying and door opening marking the end at least of this part of her journey. She heard him walking away and another door opening, vague voices fading away as it closed. She tried to relax, but the sun was now beating down on the car, with no cooling wind to counteract it. She dozed off a few times, sweat running into her eyes. Her hands were now agonising and she thought that she might lose them to gangrene if they were not released soon. After what seemed like an eternity in her own private hell, Erica heard voices and footsteps approaching the car.

"You fool!" she heard one voice hiss, vaguely familiar, but she could not place it. "Why bring her here? They will leave no stone unturned when she is found to be missing. You will bring us all down, and for worse than some ivory and rhino horn . . ."

Then she heard the Smoking Man.

"Shut up you spineless idiot!" he snarled. "My time is finished in this country anyway—I have been saving for a while and know when it is time to go. My new boss, Colonel Obija has not accepted my bribes and has now started an investigation against me."

She heard him smack the roof of the car in anger as he went on.

"I just need a week to take out the rest of the ivory and maybe some rhino horn from that damned reserve, and we will be across the border in six hours. I'll take the brat with me and dispose of her somewhere up north. She's probably worth as much as a prize pair of tusks."

"And how do you think you are going to pull that off, poaching the rest of the elephant from the reserve," sneered the quieter voice. "You think they are going to open the gates for you?"

"Exactly!" replied the Smoking Man. "When Granger gets my message that it is his daughter or the bloody elephant, who do you think he is going to choose?"

"I don't like it," came back the other voice. "There is too much risk . . ."

"I don't care what you think, old man," grated the Smoking Man. "You are as deep in this as we are, and if I or my men go down, so do you. Just remember that if you have any thoughts of talking. Now, let's get her into that nice little secret cellar of yours."

Erica blinked in the sudden light as the boot lid was popped open, and the Smoking Man reached in to pull the blind up over her eyes before she could make out anything. She was lifted as easily as a piece of baggage and carried swiftly and roughly through a doorway, banging her head as they went through. She cried out in pain and received a shaking for her trouble.

"Keep quiet!" he snapped.

She heard the other person moving something and opening another door, and then she had the sensation of going downwards, the Smoking Man grunting now with the effort of holding her in front and descending. It was immediately cooler and she thought this must be the cellar they were talking about. He dropped her unceremoniously on the floor and nudged her with his booted foot.

"Behave yourself, be quiet and do as you are told and you may survive this adventure," he said, leaning down and slicing through the cable tie with a bayonet drawn from the scabbard on his belt.

The returning blood was almost as painful as the stricture, and she whimpered out loud.

"If you so much as think about breaking out, or raising the alarm, I will tie you up again and leave you like a trussed guinea fowl. Enjoy your stay."

She heard the clatter of his boots up the stairway and the thud of the trapdoor closing, followed by the scraping sound again. She knew immediately that the trapdoor was hidden now beneath some kind of furniture and that she was well and truly locked in. She removed the blind from her eyes and was thankful for the dim light burning behind a wire cage in the roof of the cellar. Rubbing the circulation back into her wrists, Erica turned around slowly, taking in the contents of the dank and cool bunker. There were various crates stacked against one wall, with some old carpets rolled up and tied in bundles. Some drums were stacked in one corner. She quietly climbed the wooden steps to the trapdoor and tried pushing upward, but it did not budge an inch.

"Must be locked as well as having something placed on top," she mused, looking around for any other avenue of escape. Apart from the trapdoor, there were no windows, just four blank walls, cut from the raw earth. No bricks or plaster lined the walls and the floor was made up of loose garden pavers laid close together, at least keeping her off the earthen floor.

"Where am I?" she asked herself, at the same time knowing pretty well exactly where she was. She had placed the anxious voice as being that of Mr Bamjee, and had figured out that this was either in or near his house or store, or somewhere close by in Rafinga. At least she was on familiar ground.

"Or beneath it," she said ruefully to herself. She untied and unrolled the smallest of the carpets, intending to use it as a bed, and hauled over one of the empty crates to use as a chair. Erica sat on the crate and tried to order her thoughts. She knew she was in deep trouble and it could only get worse. She had overheard Smoking Man's plan to take her out of the country after blackmailing her father into holding back on patrols, and knew she had to escape before that happened. She had a vague idea of her fate if she was taken over the border, and none of it bore thinking about. As she pondered, Erica became aware that the air in the cellar was fresh and seemed to be moving slightly. Getting up and walking slowly around the room, she looked carefully up into the edges where the concrete ceiling met the walls and was rewarded with the sight of a plastic grating over a hole about the size of a soup bowl. When she stood on tiptoe with her face toward the grating, she could feel a definite breeze coming down. It was a vent of some kind.

"Maybe with one of those wind-driven roof fans pushing air down here", she thought to herself. "But too small to consider any kind of escape through, unless I can do an Alice in Wonderland trick . . ."

She pulled over another crate and reached up to the grate, pulling it easily away from four tiny screws holding it in place. A few bits of fluff and dust drifted down on her as she peered up the pipe, seeing a glimmer of light at the top, but not the sky.

"So, it looks like one of those funny vents with a fin on that keeps the mouth of the vent into the wind," she thought, listening to the faint sound of the vent hood rotating back and forth. She wondered about lighting a fire, dismissing that as silly, as she would be dead long before anyone came to the rescue, even if they saw the smoke. And there was the small matter of not having anything to make a fire with in the first place.

"Well, at least I can try and call Martin, even though it is a long way. He said it could be done if you concentrate, and he should be a bit closer now as he was going to come over to the station side of the reserve to meet me . . ."

She focused her whole mind on the circle of light at the top of the vent, screwing her eyes in effort as she projected a cry for help to her Brother Elephant. She got no message in reply, but felt better and decided to do it again at least every hour. She also tried to project into her father's mind, but knew he would be doing everything in his power to find her no matter what she did.

Erica sat down again on the crate, trying not to despair, breathing deeply but evenly and holding the panic at bay. Suddenly, she heard the scrape of furniture and squeal of the trapdoor and the light went out at the same time. A voice, muffled by something floated down.

"Turn around and face the wall away from the steps, close your eyes and do not move." The voice hissed. "I have brought you a chemical toilet and some water. There will be food later . . ."

Erica could not help herself and cried out, "Oh, please, please let me go, I won't say anything to anyone. You can't leave me with the Smoking Man."

"Smoking? . . . Oh, yes, him—I am afraid nobody crosses that one. Just resign yourself to your fate. Now stop talking to me and do not turn around until I have left . . ."

Erica heard the noises of her keeper's departure and the light came on again, to reveal a small camping toilet and a large plastic bottle of water at the base of the stairs. Thankfully she took several deep swallows of water and moved the toilet over to one corner, behind the stack of small drums. All she could do now was wait. And take any opportunity to escape. She felt drained and lay down on the carpet, falling asleep after fitful dreams.

Wilson met Rob Granger at the gates to the station, wringing his hands and with tears streaming down his face.

"Miss Erica! Miss Erica! She gone, oh Mr Rob, she gone!"

When Granger had calmed Wilson down enough to get a coherent story from him, he turned to the rest of the team who had gathered around with concern on their faces.

"Right, we know where she was going and when. Let's spread out on and either side of the track to Erica's Kopje. Maybe she fell and hurt herself. Keep an eye out for spoor. Let's go!"

Every single able-bodied man and most of the women who had heard, immediately set out towards the small hill, forming a line across the track and into the bush on either side. It was Tswane, who had appointed himself chief tracker and was on the road itself, keeping an eye on the sweep line, who spotted Erica's fateful encounter.

"Mr Rob!" he called. "Here—these are Erica's prints, all of us would recognise her tennis shoes anywhere," pointing with the slender stick he always carried. "And here, and here—five men at least, all wearing army issue boots, except for this one—he is much bigger and has crepe soles, maybe a more expensive shoe. It looks like a scuffle here," he said, indicating where Erica had been almost pulled off her feet. "And they set off in that direction. Like a herd of stupid buffalo—they have left a highway for us to follow," and he started out on that tireless hunter's jog that could cover a hundred miles in a day.

The rest of the team started to follow, but Granger stopped them. "No point a whole army of us blundering through the bush," he held a quick meeting with the group, breaking them up into smaller sections. Ngubane was to return to the station and take control there, with four of the rangers. They swopped radios so that the tracking team had the freshest and best sets. The last small group were to take the Land Rover and get on to the main road, which was where the tracks were heading toward, also carrying radios. Ngubane would relay and coordinate the teams from the base radio station. Mufara was left standing aside when all the dispositions were made, looking grim and angry.

"Mufara, you come with us," he pointed to Tswane, "Keep an eye out for Tswane, he will be concentrating on the ground and may not see danger elsewhere."

Mufara brightened up and quickly joined Tswane, staying a few steps behind and off to one side. Granger and the remaining three men spread out in a 'V' formation behind the tracker and they started off again, running as fast as their strength would allow. As Tswane had contemptuously pointed out, there seemed to be no attempt to anti-track by the five men and a girl. He did not hesitate even over hard ground, and within a few hours they reached the main fence where the hastily made repairs to a large hole were obvious. A small fragment of what looked like blue t-shirt clung to the sharp end of a cut wire. They cut through the same hole and found themselves at the lay-bye that now only showed a few of the fugitive spoor and a mix of tyre tracks.

It was hopeless. Dozens of vehicles stopped every day at the picnic spots, and it would be impossible to say which one may have carried Erica away. Granger called the base and asked Ngubane to send the Land Rover to pick them up.

"They are already there, or close by, over," he reported. "I have had them patrolling up and down the main road to our south boundary and back."

As he signed off, Granger could see the reserve Land Rover crest the rise and accelerate towards them. The whole team scoured the parking area for clues, emptying the rubbish bin and crawling under the concrete table and chairs, but found nothing except rubbish and voracious ants.

"The good news, if there is any, is that Erica is still alive and apparently well," Granger briefed his men. "There was no blood, and her spoor, Tswane tells me, shows she was still strong up to this point. What we don't know is what the heck is going on. Unless any of you have any different ideas, I think we should return to base, get the Police involved and hope to God . . ." he almost broke down and choked at this point, but stood up straighter and said, "We *will* find her. She is my everything."

They climbed aboard the truck and headed back to the base where Granger got hold of the Member in Charge of the Police at Rafinga, who was shocked but calm and promised to get the machinery rolling, starting with visits to nearby army bases, and road blocks on all routes leading away from the reserve, right up to the borders of the country. He notified all border posts and every police station in the country with a description of Erica and brief outline of the known facts.

Less than two hundred metres from the Police station, Erica lay uncomfortably on a musty carpet . . .

Martin crossed the reserve in record time, his shambling run belying the speed of his advance. He was confused and hurt inside from the deaths of his kin and the terrible injuries to his cousin, now tended by others from the scattered herd. He knew they would probably set out slowly for the elephant graveyard soon, supporting the wounded young bull between them. He was also concerned that he had not heard from Erica, and felt something was wrong. As he finally approached Erica's Kopje, he started picking up scents that increased his alarm. The faint but unmistakeable reek of gun oil, a whiff of unwashed humans, and something familiar . . . Ah! It was that cigarette butt Erica had shown him. Then, even fresher, the smell of Granger and his team, probably no more than a few hours before.

"What on earth is going on?" he asked himself, "There is too much happening at the same time . . ." He came across the tracks, now doubled by Granger and his team, of Erica's presence. Following them, he came, as had all the others, to the repaired breach in the main fence. His feeling of disquiet grew into despair and he turned slowly around, pondering his next move. He had almost started the long walk back when he heard, or sensed faintly on the wind Erica's thin voice, laced with fear.

"Martin, please hear me, oh please hear me. I am in so much trouble. If you are getting this, I am being held prisoner in a basement in Rafinga, probably something to do with Mr Bamjee's store . . ."

Martin gathered himself up, his great chest visibly swelling as he projected a super-strong thought across the distance between them, "I hear you, Erica. I hear you. Hang on, I will be with you as soon as I can."

He had absolutely no idea what he was going to do, but he was going to do something that he knew would put him in the face of danger. Breaking out of the reserve was easy—the fence was just an annoyance to elephants, and they knew it defined a normally safe zone. A couple of shoves, a bit of tusking and some trampling and stomping would see him on the road. The problem was he was sure to be spotted, and if he resisted being herded back into the reserve would probably be shot as a rogue elephant for the 'safety of people'. No, he would have to think it through and find a way of getting to her as clandestinely as possible. He walked the fence line down to the bottom boundary, where it turned away from the national road and cut towards the mountains. The boundary was shared here with farmland on the other side, and he could see by the poor grass and lack of trees the damage done by poor farming practices over the years. In comparison, the reserve was still a paradise of nature, with a balance between the eaters and the eaten.

Although Martin did not know where Rafinga actually was, he knew more or less how far it was by the time it took Granger or the others to drive there and back. It could not be more than a day's walk if they could do it, as he had observed, in a few hours. It was obvious that the road led there, so if he kept it on his left side he would surely meet other roads leading to the village. He started to rock one of the sturdy fence poles, pushing with his forehead and pulling with his trunk.

Rob Granger had not slept for nearly two days. His eyes were red-rimmed and his chin badly shaven. He knew he could not collapse and had to present a strong figure for Wilson and the rest of the people on the station who loved Erica as their own, but he was becoming frantic with worry. The Police had not had a whisper from the bulletins sent out, the army bases had nothing unusual to report, and pointed out that several surplus stores around the country sold army-issue boots by the hundreds, all bearing the same figure-8 pattern on the sole.

Ngubane was morose and could not help Granger snap out of his sorrow. Mufara had been very quiet, but had made several visits to Erica's Kopje with his mobile phone, noted by Ngubane who said nothing but kept watching.

Then came a call from the main gate. An envelope addressed to Granger had been dropped off by the northern run supply truck. The gate guard had asked the driver who had given him the letter, and he said it had been handed to him by an 'umfaan', a small child, in Rafinga who had not said anything. Ngubane rushed to the gate in the Land Rover and was back within minutes. Granger ripped open the envelope and withdrew a single sheet of school lined paper. His face went white and he staggered into his office, closing the door behind him. He slumped into his chair and read again the message, printed in a crude scrawl:

> We have your daughter. Do not call the police. Do not try to find her or she will die. You will hold back all patrols for the next two weeks. You will not follow up on any reports. If you do these things you may see your little girl again. If you do not, you will be responsible for what happens.

"Oh God," Granger moaned, realising what the message meant. "They want free rein in the reserve for two weeks. They will decimate the elephant and get to the rhino as well."

He became aware of the insistent knocking on the door. It was Ngubane with a look of deep concern on his face.

"What is it, Rob? What's going on?"

Granger realised he could not keep this from Ngubane. He would need to know why the patrols were being pulled and follow-up operations stopped. He tossed the letter across the desk and watched as Ngubane scanned it, his eyebrows rising and a scowl transforming his face.

"Bastards!" he spat. "Whatever your decision, I am with you. How can you balance your daughter against the animals?"

"It goes much deeper than that Ngubane," he replied, realising the true implications of the demand. "If I agree, not only do I endanger every animal in this supposed place of sanctuary, but I also betray my own sacred trust to protect them, to do the job I am employed to do, and by God, my own self-worth. How could I look in a mirror again knowing I had a hand in mass slaughter?" He covered his face with his hands. "And yet, I cannot lose Erica. She is all I have, all I care about before this reserve and the people and animals in it."

Ngubane came around the desk and put his hand on Granger's shoulder. "As I said—you make the decisions, I'll back you. All the way."

"Thanks, Ngubane. I need to think this through. Give me a little time."

Ngubane quietly closed the door behind him.

Erica woke from a half-dream, thinking she had heard Martin and wondering if it was in fact only a dream.

"No, that was what woke me," she said firmly to herself, trying to dispel the fear that she was lost forever.

Bamjee, or someone else with the muffled voice, had brought some sandwiches, made she noted, by the café on main street (they were still wrapped in cellophane with the price tag—not so clever, Mr B!). She still had plenty of water and her bodily needs were taken care of. It was her mind that she needed to control and keep positive. She had nothing to read or do except think of ways of escape, about her past, her mother and father, her friends and family, and of course her new brother, Martin. At least they left the light on—she felt she would give up hope in the pitch darkness of this lonely hole in the ground.

10. Searching For Erica

Martin trampled the thick strands of wire to the ground. Four fence poles had been snapped off, and blood oozed down his forehead where broken wire ends had cut deeply, but he had created a path across the fence line and was about to set foot in forbidden territory. There was little cover on this piece of farmland and he knew it was likely that he would be seen and the alarm raised. A herd of cattle shifted uneasily as he passed by, their long horns dipping, dust coiling up around their nervous hooves. A small dog yapped loudly but did not work up the courage to do more. There did not seem to be a herder with the animals apart from the little watch dog, and Martin moved on. He came upon another fence, but only the normal farm five-strand barbed wire with wooden droppers that folded like paper beneath his feet. Yet another fence, and another—it seemed that the farm had been divided into paddocks, creating a never-ending series of annoying barriers.

Eventually he reached a better-constructed fence and realised it was the boundary between farms. He could see on the other side of the fence a crop of maize with a neatly cut fire-break line separating the two properties. It seemed to Martin that this farm was better run than the one he was leaving, with large stands of natural forest left between the cultivated fields. Where the fields were fallow, good grass cover had taken hold, protecting the soil and no doubt providing food for the farm animals. In the far distance he could see a farmhouse, neatly laid out and ringed by mature shady camel thorn trees. Green lawns surrounded the homestead, and the barns and outbuildings were painted and in good repair.

It was late afternoon and Martin decided to lie up in one of the wooded patches where there was cover, and a small stream running through. He had to eat and drink no matter how urgent his journey. Elephants need to refuel regularly to maintain strength from the poor quality of the leaves and bark they eat, and water in large quantities is essential for the digestion process. Martin found some browsing amongst the trees and also helped himself to a few trunk twists of maize stalks, knowing at the same time he was probably doing something wrong. But, they sure tasted good. After a long drink at the stream, he moved more deeply into the thicket and settled down for the night, first sending a message to Erica. There was no response and he started dozing and gathering strength for the coming day.

Back at the reserve base, Rob Granger was holding a meeting with the Member in Charge of the Police from Rafinga, a senior Criminal Investigation Department Officer from the city, and Ngubane. No trace of Erica had been found, and the Criminal Investigation Department Officer was sceptical about the chances of a quick solution.

"With every hour we don't find her, the potential search zone expands by fifty to eighty miles. Within 24 hours, that puts us outside most of the borders of this country. Our best bet is someone talking. Everything is seen, somewhere along the line, and someone knows something that will lead us to her . . ."

"That's all very well Chief Inspector, but we cannot go public and alert the kidnappers that we are breaking the terms of the demand they sent," replied Granger.

"I agree," responded the plain-clothes man, "And we will, for the time being, extend every resource we have in the crime underworld, put pressure on our informants and stir up the bad guys until they get so tired of us that someone whispers in our ears."

Ngubane remained silent, looking from speaker to speaker and making notes. He was keeping a diary of events and typing it up for Granger and the team to review whenever they met, hoping to spot something they may have missed.

When the police had taken their leave, Ngubane sat down with Granger and covered the main points of the meeting. He also mentioned that he had seen Mufara going to Erica's Kopje with his mobile phone several times since Erica's disappearance. Granger looked up sharply at this, but said nothing, resolving to confront Mufara later. They agreed to keep a silent watch over the reserve, with guards and trackers observing from hidden points, armed with radios.

Granger did not know what he would do when a report came in of poachers in the park, but he could not just sit on his hands and wait for the slaughter. As he glanced out of the window he saw Ngubane heading out of the gate in the direction of Erica's Kopje and wondered if he was checking on Mufara. He rose wearily and made his way to the workshop, finding Mufara busy with some paperwork. Mufara got up and greeted Granger, offering him a seat and a cup of tea which he accepted.

"If it was Erica, we would be having biscuits stolen from Wilson," Mufara tried to lighten the load bearing down on the distraught father, explaining how she would bring goodies to their tea times.

"I didn't know she was friendly with you, Mufara," said Granger. "I thought she was of the opinion that you were a bit aloof from the rest of us. It's my fault as much as anybody's I guess—I have not had time to bring you into our somewhat tight little family here at the base."

"Yes, I did have an attitude, but that has nothing to do with you, your daughter or this place," Mufara replied. "My personal circumstances are a bit difficult, but Erica helped me see things differently, and we have become friends over the past weeks."

Granger broached the subject of Mufara's frequent visits to the kopje where mobile phone reception could be found. "I don't want to pry into your private affairs, but in the circumstances, I need to know I'm covering every base in the search for my daughter . . ."

"And I am under suspicion," said Mufara with a small smile.

"Well, someone for sure has been leaking precise information from this base, you are one of few people with a mobile, you are new to the area—you do kind of stand out as a possible suspect, Mufara. But I am being up front with you, and don't really believe it was you in any event . . ."

Mufara got up from behind his desk, walked over to the door, looked out both ways and then closed it. He checked out the one window, closing it and dropping the blind before returning to his seat.

"I think it is time to come clean with you, Mr Granger. I am, as you, and Erica, have discovered not quite what I seem to be. I am at best an amateur mechanic and enjoy the tinkering. So, yes, I am a fraud and here under false pretences. We had hoped to keep my secret a secret for a little longer, but Erica's kidnapping has moved the schedule up . . ."

Granger started to rise from his seat, his face contorted with anger.

"No, no, Mr Granger. Hear me out. I am on your side. I am a special investigator attached to the Ministry of Wildlife. My job is the tracing of illegal game product sales, working from the bigger end—the people who create the market, pay the middle men and ultimately the poachers. Lately we have been receiving information about larger and larger consignments demanded by the buyers, with almost no limit on the prices. The world is running out of ivory and horn and these people know that if they can make a big coup and then sit on the stocks for a few years, they will make a hundred times the profit. We knew you would be a prime target because you run a successful reserve with good herds of protected species and you are quite close to the northern border areas. We have also been keeping an eye on suspected dealers and know something is going down, but not the who, when and where until now, when Erica has become a pawn . . ."

"But why did you not tell me who you were," Granger felt angry and hurt about being kept in the dark.

"I am really sorry, but my orders were clear. It was also for your own safety—if there is an informant and you let slip about me inadvertently, we could both have been in danger and the operation compromised. I have been putting extreme pressure on my informants about Erica, that is why I have been seen using my mobile over the last two days. I am sure she has not been moved too far away from here and that they are depending on us panicking about cross-border kidnapping and diluting the search over the whole country. You may not know it, but Erica has also been doing some detective work. I caught her going through my diary one night, and she has made some comments that lead me to think she was on the trail of something. I think we should check out her room and see if we can find anything . . ."

Granger calmed down and agreed with Mufara that Erica had been a bit furtive and busy over the past weeks. They went over to her study and Granger went through her note books while Mufara booted up her laptop and scanned the files. It took him less than five minutes to find where she had hidden her notes.

"I had better give Miss Granger some lessons in espionage when we get her back," he smiled at Granger, who had also discovered her reversed notes in the project file. They were impressed with her neat and methodical notes on all the staff, and her diary of thoughts, suspicions and discoveries led them to find the two cigarette butts amongst her collection on the shelf.

"Who is this Martin she mentioned once or twice?" asked Mufara.

"Not a clue," responded Granger. "She also blurted that name out when I told her about the shooting that night."

"What do you notice about her review of staff?" asked Mufara.

"Well, I see she has left out Wilson, Ngubane and, thank goodness, me," he responded.

"And rightly so. She must be able to trust someone, and you are an obvious. And Wilson, who I believe has been with you for many years. She also seems to trust Ngubane implicitly and I guess we should respect that. But I am a detective, and everybody is a suspect until I say so," he said, making a small joke of his position.

"I see she had a run-in with Bamjee," Mufara said, pointing to her diary entry.

"Yes, she did not know that Bamjee and I have had dealings and are not on good terms. She apparently wandered into his shop and bought a few things, nothing more to it . . ."

"I think there is more to it," he replied. "She may have told you it was an accidental meeting, but here she mentions he got angry when she asked for some illegal ivory jewellery—did she mention that to you?"

"No, she did not, and I would probably have punished her for trying to entrap someone if she had," he replied, at the same time mentally applauding his plucky daughter in her attempts to find out who was behind the poaching.

"And this 'Smoking Man' she mentions—all we know about him is that he is big, wears fancy clothes and has serious sunglasses. I wonder where he fits in, apart from a bit of a tenuous link between the cigarette butts at the kopje and one she picked up in town?"

Mufara paged down, but there was little more information to be had. He printed out the whole document and shut down the computer.

"I think you should lock this laptop, her notes and the evidence in the safe," he said to Granger, glancing down at the cigarette butts. "Those may be more important than we think if it comes down to DNA testing at some stage."

Mufara promised to up the surveillance on Bamjee and to circulate the description of the Smoking Man, and he left immediately for Erica's Kopje. Granger felt somehow more hopeful now that he had some pegs to hang his fears and suspicions on, and he decided to go into Rafinga to be closer to the search centre. He would stay in Fran's house and keep a low profile but be more available to calls from the Police than by the unsecure radio network used at the base.

Leaving Ngubane in charge, he left as soon as he could, arriving in Rafinga in darkness and putting the station wagon behind the garage and out of sight from the street. Not that it would do much good. In a village like Rafinga, it didn't take long for everyone to know who was doing what, and just switching on the low lights in the living room would have been noted by the neighbours and probably reported to the Police.

Sure enough, an hour later there was a knock on the door and a young constable stood on the step, torch at the ready.

"Oh, it is you, Mr Granger. Sorry to disturb, but we have been asked to keep an eye on your sister-in-law's house. Is everything in order?"

Granger grinned at the policeman and assured him that all was well and that he would be in the house for a few days. He said he would be visiting the Member in Charge the following day and thanked him for doing his duty so diligently.

He fell asleep reviewing Erica's notes for the hundredth time. Who was Martin? What was the Smoking Man up to? Where is my daughter?

11. The Search Narrows

Erica, her father and Martin all woke around the same time, each feeling lost and powerless, and none knowing where the others were. Erica's only clue as to the time was the weak light filtering down through the vent in the corner of the cellar. Her father was woken by the barking of dogs and greying sky of dawn. Martin had been dozing on and off throughout the night and had also started to the distant sound of dogs yapping at the farm homestead. He set off before the sun rose completely, hoping to avoid detection over the next open piece of ground, but the dogs must have caught his scent and were now frantically howling and barking.

Martin saw lights come on in the house and spill through the front door as the farmer came out, wearing pyjamas, a rifle clearly discernible in his hands. The man shouted something at the dogs and shone a powerful torch around the yard, probably thinking that a jackal or mongoose had got into the hen house near the barn. After checking the yard, he shut the dogs in the barn and went back inside the house.

Martin breathed a sigh of relief and moved on again, hurrying for the next copse of trees. Before he made it, he saw another person come out of the house, a younger man or boy, fully dressed and also carrying a rifle. The young man walked over to a shed and emerged riding a motorcycle, the rifle slung over his shoulder. The puttering sound of the machine faded as they rode over the rise towards the maize fields.

It was Nick van Heerden on the trail bike, and he was on his way to check on crop raiders: baboon, warthog and kudu all dearly loved the taste of unripe corn on the cob. His father had got him out of bed and instructed him to patrol the farm boundary and ensure the fences were undamaged before coming back for breakfast.

It was bitterly cold in the early morning on the bike and Nick had forgotten to put on a jacket. Tears streamed from the corners of his eyes and his knuckles had turned blue, but he loved this time of the day and rode on, savouring the freshness and colours of the sky, now a deep blue tinged with salmon pink as the sun made its endless journey from night to day.

He almost missed the place where Martin had flattened the fence, as it had sprung back into place once he stepped off the strands of wire, but two of the posts were snapped off at ground level, and of course there were the dustbin lid tracks leading away down the firebreak between the fields. He almost fell off in surprise but recovered and set the bike on its stand, examining the tracks in awe. He had never seen an elephant on the farm, but his father had told him that in the "olden days" they regularly broke through the fences in herd strength, trying to repeat their ancient migration paths that often covered hundreds of miles. That was before the game reserve had been proclaimed and measures put in place to protect both the farmers and the wildlife, but conflict still arose on the farms bordering the reserve. Lion, at best lazy and cunning hunters, sometimes broke through and snacked on a few cows or donkeys, immediately claimed as being "prize breeding stock" by a wily farmer looking for compensation, even if they were scrubby old bush cattle and wild donkeys. Cheetah too did not always respect the imposed boundaries, and of course hyena and jackal were considered vermin by most farmers.

Nick followed the tracks on foot, leaving the bike where it was. His rifle was too light to even consider using it on anything bigger than a warthog, but he clutched it tightly as he walked. He found the place where Martin had helped himself to a bunch of maize stalks, a trail of leaves and chewed pith leading him to the wooded copse where he had spent the night.

"The Old Man is going to poo himself over this," Nick thought to himself. "A few mealie stalks isn't going to break the bank, but I bet he goes ape when I tell him."

Nick almost wished he could leave out the small damage to the crop, but knew his father would be up here like lightening to verify the unlikely story his son was going to tell him. He followed the tracks out to the other side of the copse, where he could see the farm house down the gentle slope of the valley. Smoke drifted from the kitchen chimney and he knew his mother would be preparing breakfast.

"A breakfast I am unlikely to enjoy today," was his rueful thought. His father would not wait around for mere eating when his precious farm was under attack.

The trail led towards the next wooded area which was close to their southern boundary, and unconsciously Nick wished the elephant would get out of the area before his father did something stupid. He walked slowly back to the motor bike and equally slowly puttered back to the farm, parking the machine back under the shed, unloading his rifle and entering through the kitchen door. He put his rifle in the safe and thankfully wrapped his hands around the mug of coffee offered by his mother, her kind eyes filled with concern at the chattering of his teeth and wind-reddened cheeks.

"Don't worry Mom," he said cheerfully, "my fault for not wearing a jacket, and it really is great out there. Have I got something to tell you!"

His father walked in, now dressed for his day on the farm, khaki shorts and shirt, rugby socks and veldskoene, the hardy shoes of the bush, often made from kudu skin. His floppy hat dangled from one large hand and his huge size dominated the room.

"So, what did you find?" he grunted at Nick. "Or were you so cold you could not see the end of your nose? If you don't have the sense to dress properly, how can I rely on you to do anything else?"

"Well, Pa, maybe I was a bit cold, but I know elephant tracks when I see them, and we have an elephant on the farm, or at least passing through. He came through the fence near the big Mopani tree on Smith's place, went down to the river in the small forest and looks like he spent the night there, leaving before light this morning. The dogs must have caught his scent as he passed to the south. I have not seen him, but the spoor is fresh," Nick gave his report, leaving out a few things.

"The devil you say!" exclaimed his father. "You sure, boy?"

"Like I said, Pa, I know what I see, and anyway you are going to go out and check on me, so you can see for yourself."

"You getting cheeky with me, boy?" Van Heerden stared into Nick's face, looking for the defiance he felt sometimes lurked below the surface. He loved his only son, and wanted the best for him, but he had to have discipline if he was to take over the farm when the time was right.

"Show me where you saw this thing. Let's go," he strode towards the door, grabbing the Jeep keys off the hook near the door.

"What about his breakfast, dear?" asked Mrs van Heerden as Nick rose to leave.

"Ag, that can wait. We won't die. I want to see what he is talking about. We will not be long."

Nick looked at his mother and shrugged his shoulders, smiling at her as he followed his father out to the old Jeep. Climbing aboard and letting two of the dogs jump in the back, they set off back up the valley, Nick directing his father first to the breach in the fence and then down the firebreak towards the wooded area.

"Verdomp!" Van Heerden shouted, going visibly red in the face when he saw the damage to the maize on the side of the track. "He is destroying my mealies! We will have to shoot him immediately!"

"Come on, Pa. It is only a half-dozen stalks. He did not even walk through the maize field—that would have been something worth shouting about. Besides, you know you can't go round shooting elephant or any protected game without permission from the wildlife people."

Van Heerden turned to his son with a stunned look on his florid face.

"Are you telling me you don't mind the destruction this beast has brought to our farm," he demanded. "You care nothing for the money we spent on seeds and equipment, the worry of the rain, the bloody baboons and pig, the thieves at the co-op, and you say it is nothing?"

"Pretty much, yes," said Nick calmly. "It really is nothing. A few hours to patch the fences, a handful of mealie stalks, some interesting spoor and a few really big elephant poops. He will be gone from our farm in a few hours if he keeps going in that direction, so I guess there will be another fence needing some attention, but for my part, I think it is exciting that elephant still live and walk on these lands, and we should just let him be. Report him to the wildlife officer in Rafinga or to Mr Granger at the reserve, but let it go . . ."

Van Heerden fumed silently for a few seconds, trying to come to terms with his son's new-found courage to stand up to him and to refute his argument with his own infallible version of what was right.

"Ja, well, maybe, but we track him out of our farm before I make a decision," he grumpily thrust the Jeep into gear and they started skirting the fields to come around to the direction Nick was sure the elephant was taking.

They crossed the spoor every now and then, sometimes having to detour for a mile or more where the Jeep could not follow. Eventually they came out of an old cut line at their southern boundary fence and slowly drove along the fire break road, looking for a sign. They found it where they thought they would, in almost a direct line from where the animal had entered the northern part of the farm. The fence was again broken, but standing up, suspended by its wires that had not snapped when Martin pushed the fence droppers over and walked across to the next farm, owned by the hermit-like Oujan Erasmus.

"He seems to be on a mission," said Nick to his father. "No deviation, just a straight line from wherever to who knows where. I just hope he will be okay and not get into too much trouble."

"Well, if trouble is what he is looking for, he is going to get it," muttered Van Heerden. "I'm going to 'phone Erasmus and tell him he has an unwanted guest on his farm. Let him sort it out."

They drove back to the farm house in silence, Van Heerden's fingers drumming restlessly on the steering wheel, Nick thinking of ways to warn the elephant off Erasmus's land. The old man was unpredictable and irritable, as Nick had once found out when he went for a walk that went a little further than their own farm boundary. He had waved an old shotgun in the air, accused Nick of any number of crimes and chased him off the farm, shouting all the while. Nick thought he was pretty harmless but had not stopped to argue.

While he was enjoying his late breakfast he heard his father on the telephone to Erasmus, telling him about the elephant 'invasion'.

"An invasion of one," he muttered to himself.

"What was that, dear?" his mother asked as she tidied up the kitchen table.

"Nothing, Ma," he replied, "Tell Pa I'm going to check the whole farm fence line, be back this afternoon. Don't wait for me for lunch, I'll take some biltong and water . . ."

Nick quickly packed some of the dried game meat and a water bottle into his small rucksack and took off on the motor bike, heading for the southern part of the farm. There was an old cattle gate between their and Erasmus's property, used when cattle strayed either side and had to be herded back. He drove through and re-locked the gate, now driving on the opposite side and looking for the place where Martin had crossed. Once he was at the place they had seen earlier, he turned off and followed the tracks across the grassy plain. Erasmus grew only a few hectares of maize for his own use and the farm was basically a cattle ranch, undeveloped and still quite wild in places. Nick had no problem following Martin's tracks for most of the way, and was impressed with the distance Martin had covered since morning. He puzzled over the reason for the lone elephant taking off from the safety of the reserve and thought that he should have called Erica or Mr Granger before leaving the farm house.

He could see through the trees and bush Erasmus's shabby dwelling, consisting of badly plastered walls of mud brick and old tin roofing. Several derelict trucks and a tractor lay in pieces around the house, weeds growing up through the skeletal remains. An old Chev truck seemed to be the only probable working thing, as all the tyres were pumped up and there were no weeds or grass taking over. He decided to call on the old man and ask to use his 'phone. He could not get hold of the reserve base by normal telephone, but could call the Police who could patch him through on radio or at least pass on the message.

He swung towards the house, finding a proper but overgrown farm road cutting across his path and leading down to where he could see Erasmus emerging from his front door to investigate the sound of the motor bike. As usual, he had his trusty shotgun clenched in his bony fist, the other hand shading his pale blue eyes as he struggled to identify the invader.

"What do you want? Who sent you? This is private property," were his words of greeting as Nick dismounted and kicked the side stand down.

"I'm Nick," he said, walking slowly toward the old man, showing both his empty hands. "Nick van Heerden, you know, from next door. My father was on the telephone to you just now about the elephant . . ."

"Oh yes, I know you. You trespassed on my farm last year and I chased you off. You were up to no good then, and I want to know what you are up to now. But, I'm busy—I have an elephant to shoot, but I can't find my big gun. Did you steal it?"

"No Mr Erasmus, I did not steal anything, then or now. I am tracking the elephant and wanted to use your telephone to call the Police in Rafinga so they can alert the reserve and send a team to deal with it. Is that okay with you?"

"Ja, and who is going to pay for the call, hey? You think you can just walk in here and waste my money . . ." Nick, exasperated, cut him off in mid-sentence.

"The telephone exchange will not charge for an emergency call to the Police, and even if they do, I'll tell them to bill it to our account, not yours," he started for the dilapidated front door with the old man trailing behind, muttering all the while.

The telephone was in the usual place as most farm houses, on the wall near the front door, normally the entrance hall, but this house was not big enough to entertain such luxuries and the instrument was just fixed to the wall on the left of the doorway. Nick picked up the handset and cranked the handle, first listening to see if anyone else was busy on the line. The familiar voice of the exchange operator came on, asking for the number.

"Hi Mrs Dabenga, it is Nick here, at Mr Erasmus's farm. Could you put me through to the Police station, or patch me through to the radio network at the reserve base . . ."

"Eeh! I don't think Mr Erasmus's 'phone has been used for six months—that one is so stingy I'm sure he steams stamps off envelopes and sticks them back on his own mail. I can't put you through to the radio network, there is a panic of some sort going on, but wait. I know Mr Granger is in town. Let me try his sister in law's house."

There was a crackling pause while she transferred the line to the automatic exchange and then the normal ring tone. The 'phone was answered on the second ring, startling Nick by the abrupt, almost angry reply that resounded in his ear.

"Yes, who is it?"

"I—I am Nick. Nick van Heerden, Mr Granger," he stuttered.

"Yes, Nick, of course. I am sorry to have shouted at you. We have a terrible problem going on. Erica is missing and we believe she has been kidnapped. Do you know anything?"

Nick was shattered at the news and could say nothing for a few seconds.

"No, Mr Granger, this is the first I have heard. My God, what is going on. How can I help?"

Granger told Nick everything that he knew, knowing he was a friend of Erica's and would at least be another pair of eyes on their side.

"Why did you call, Nick, and how did you know where to find me?" Granger asked when he had finished.

"Well, finding you was easy as Mrs Dabenga at the exchange, and the reason I was calling was to tell you about an elephant that crossed our farm last night. He is now on this farm, Mr Erasmus's place, but heading south at a fast pace. I am worried that he will get into trouble if he causes any damage. Already Mr Erasmus is already looking for his 'big gun'."

"Okay, Nick, thanks for that. I'll get hold of Ngubane and get him to despatch a team in a vehicle to get on the trail and try and persuade him to go back. It is a serious situation for any so called rogue elephants. Doing a darting and transport operation is costly, and if he causes trouble the only option may be to put him down . . ." Granger sadly outlined the possible outcome.

"Tell that old Erasmus I'll have him arrested if he so much as points a gun at that animal—he's more likely to wound it and then we really will have a problem."

"I will keep following him, Mr Granger. Tell your team to look out for me on the red Honda scrambler bike. I am wearing a blue denim shirt and a green baseball cap. I'll see where he crosses Road 2309 which is where I last saw him heading and wait for them if I find something," Nick offered the only help he could think of.

"That would be great, Nick, thanks. I am really tied up with Erica's disappearance, but life does have to go on. Please let me know as soon as you are home and you are safe. Do not approach the elephant at all. It sounds like he may have gone a bit crazy, maybe because of the shooting a few days ago . . ."

They rang off, not hearing the gentle click of the exchange operator who had listened (as she did most of the day) to every word. Kidnapping! Wild Elephants! This was real news and far more exciting than Mr Blignaut being seen leaving Mrs Jameson's house in the early morning whilst Mr Jameson was on business in the city . . .

Within an hour everyone in town who had been told not to tell anyone else knew the whole story, or at least ten different and increasingly lurid versions of the story. From White Slavers to Pirates of the Caribbean, rabid elephants clearing a path for man-eating lions, this was heady stuff for the sleepy hollow of Rafinga.

News took little time to reach Bamjee, always at the centre of his web of information and possible opportunity. He was not interested in the wild animal stories, but the breaking of the news about Erica was what he had been dreading. He had never agreed to the plan, and could see no good coming from any of it, but he was in the clutches of the implacable Major Mugani, a known killer with absolutely no conscience. He had been running poaching, gold and diamond smuggling schemes for years, lining his Swiss bank accounts and bribing, coercing or blackmailing people in every walk of life. From high in the wildlife ministry down to lowly Police constables, many were in his pay, debt or outright fear. Bamjee knew his days were numbered with the appointment of an honest Army commander who knew what was going on but was having a hard time proving it. Investigators in the Army and several ministries were working full time on the cases, but met with many blank walls, missing documents and outright lies. When Mugani finally toppled, there was going to be an avalanche of people trying to escape the fallout.

Bamjee had already transferred most of his cash to a distant cousin near the Pakistan border with Afghanistan, completely untraceable and safe as could be. His air ticket to London was already booked, with an open date for the next six months. His wife had already left to set up home in a quiet cul-de-sac in Eastleigh, south of London. A bag lay packed and ready to go at all times, and a new set of identification documents, complete with British visa, was in the safe. A shave of the beard, change into Western clothes, and he would be another person and good to go.

His grasping and ne'er do well brother and his whining brood could have the store, which no doubt would be run into the ground within six months, not that he cared. The store did make a profit, but had always been just a cover for his various illegal business transactions. He was tired of standing behind the counter, smiling, nodding and agreeing with customers who complained about everything, including his prices (which were the best in town). The only big fly in this particular jar of ointment was Mugani. If he timed his escape badly, the big man would track him down and snap his scrawny neck as easily as a Sunday Madras chicken.

Whilst Bamjee pondered his options, Erica was, no more than thirty paces away, pacing her prison cell. She was feeling dirty, hungry and downhearted. Powerless to do more than try and keep sane, she tried to visualise what her father, Martin and Ngubane were doing to find her. She did not know whether the Police or anybody else was involved or if they had found any clues. She knew her father well enough to know they would have found the tracks leading to the fence after her abduction, and the small scrap of her shirt that she had deliberately allowed to rip on a piece of wire as she passed through, but how would they follow on from there?

Suddenly Martin's voice came to her, much stronger than before.

"I am close, Erica. I can hear the traffic on the main road and smell the stink of many humans in one place, and burning rubbish. Do you smell the same thing?"

"Oh, Martin, thank goodness. I thought you had deserted me or been hurt. Yes, I think what you smell is the village dump site. They burn once a week, and if the wind is wrong, it really is ripe," she replied.

She tried to visualise the village layout in relation to where the dump was and asked Martin which direction the wind was coming from.

"The south-east," he replied.

"That means you will reach the dump site before the town, as it is on the road to the coast, on the north-west side of town," she worked out his general position and thought about how he could approach without using the roads.

"If you go around the dump on the right side you will be in the 'town-lands' or municipal property. It is still pretty much bush area with no fences and you can get right up to the town limits without using a main road. You will come across the railway line and then after that there is no cover, so you should try and hide out until dark before crossing . . ."

He agreed with her and told her he would call again when he was in a more secure position. He had heard the same motor bike that had been on his trail from the first farm, intermittently droning up and down the road he had crossed some time before, and knew his time of freedom was limited.

Nick had met up with the tracking team from the reserve and shown them where Martin had crossed the road. It was too rough for the Land Rover to follow directly, and they decided to loop around to the railway line and patrol up and down the service road looking for sign. Nick however was able to follow the tracks, standing up on the foot pegs, sometimes riding right over rocks and old tree trunks with the rugged bike.

Rob Granger was at the Police station, sitting in the Member in Charge's office. The Criminal Investigation Department Detective Officer was there, and it was clear that none of them had slept well. No firm news had been received, but some informants had wind of a big consignment of ivory that would be leaving sometime soon. Attempts to get more information had been unsuccessful, and one potential informant had been found with his head facing in the wrong direction in a dark and dirty alley in the city.

Back at the reserve station, Ngubane had surreptitiously followed Mufara to Erica's Kopje, waiting for him to disappear over the rock formation at the top before silently snaking his way up from the opposite side, stopping just short of the overhang, well out of sight. He could hear Mufara entering a number into a mobile 'phone, the soft beeps carrying clearly. Hearing only one side of the conversation, he still managed to understand a lot of what was said, and his face hardened. He stayed hidden until he was sure Mufara was well away from the hill, and then quietly slid down and walked back in the lengthening shadows of the early evening.

12. Good and Evil

Nick van Heerden came careering around a formation of huge granite boulders, putting one foot down to control the skid in the suddenly soft sand, he found himself face to face with a huge bull elephant, dried blood crusted on a forehead framed by enormous ragged ears and bracketed by a pair of long white tusks. He let the bike fall to the ground, trapping one leg under the frame, knowing his last moments had come. Lying in the sand looking up at his destiny, his thoughts were on what his father would have to say about this, his last and most foolish action.

Martin stepped forward a few paces, looking down at the boy who had chased him for most of this strange day, wondering what to do to stop him without hurting him. He saw that the motor bike had trapped Nick's leg, close to the red-hot exhaust. He reached down, wrapped his trunk around the handle bars and lifted the machine as if it were a toy, dropping it a few yards away. Nick sat up and looked into the elephant's eyes, knowing it was futile to run and wondering what it would be like to be trampled and stabbed. Would it hurt much, or would it be over so quickly one has no time to think about it?

"Of course it will hurt, you idiot," Martin had picked up his thoughts clearly, "I think a couple of broken ribs, one arm, a leg and collar bone for starters, followed by a main course of being impaled on my tusks, and for afters, a high toss over these rocks, what do you say?"

Nick was flabbergasted, he was sure he could hear the elephant talking to him, but it was impossible, he must be losing his mind in the face of his impending death.

"Well, what d'you have to say, young man. Why are you following me?"

97

"Are you really speaking to me, or am I already dead?" Nick asked, a tremor in his voice.

"If you were dead, you'd know it," replied Martin, not too sure that that made any sense, but it sounded good.

"I'm Nick van Heerden, sir. I am trying to keep you out of trouble. You are in great danger by walking through the farms and heading for villages. People will shoot you even if you do nothing."

"Aha! So you are the friend of my sister, the shy and bashful Mr Nick," Martin recalled some of his conversations with Erica about this young man, who did indeed seem to be a reasonable sort of the species.

"Your . . . what?" Nick stuttered.

"My sister, Erica—look it is a long story, and I certainly don't have time now. Erica is in real danger and I am trying to find her—why don't you go home and leave me to it," Martin started turning away.

"But, sir, I know about Erica—I spoke to her father earlier today and he told me the whole story. The poachers want two weeks in the reserve to kill all the elephant and rhino and are holding Erica to ransom unless her father agrees to hold back all patrols."

Martin turned back, ears flaring. "Then it's worse than I thought. Not only Erica but all my family and friends as well. Will you people never leave us be . . ."

"Please let me help," begged Nick, still not understanding how or why he was communicating with a wild animal. "I can go places you cannot, talk to people and report back to you. Why are you trying to get to Rafinga, do you think she is here?"

"I know she is there. We are communicating, and she knows more or less where she is, but it is underground and not going to be easy. If you really care about her, come along with me, but if you betray me, we may need to revisit the trampling, tusking and tossing thing, okay?"

He turned back towards the village and plodded on, Nick trotting behind for a few hundred yards before Martin turned back in exasperation, lifted a shocked Nick onto his back and resumed his mile-eating pace. They reached the railway line, glinting on its bed of gravel through the last of the tree line. Villagers had been illegally cutting firewood here for some years, and the natural forest was thin, the undergrowth taking over in swathes of thorny bramble. Martin moved back into the scant cover, finding a few trees growing close together where he could blend into the background and shadow.

"I'll go up ahead," offered Nick. "I can creep up to the rail service road and see for a long distance in each direction. If I see the park patrol, I can tell them you have set off in another direction—that should buy us some time . . ."

"Alright, go ahead," Martin replied, gently lifting Nick down. "I'll see if I can make contact with Erica and come up with a plan."

Nick stealthily set off in the direction of the railway line and village, wondering at the same time what his parents must be thinking. It was late afternoon and he should have been back at the house hours ago. His father would soon realise from the motor bike tracks that he had left the farm, Erasmus would confirm his direction, and the search would be on. He decided that his priority was Erica and to take his punishment later.

There was no movement on the rail service road, but fresh vehicle tracks indicated some traffic had passed during the day. He settled down behind some thick undergrowth on the verge and reflected on this strangest of days.

Martin was concentrating on Erica, projecting powerful waves towards the village, and she replied almost immediately.

"I am okay, Martin, but very scared. I think they are preparing to move me at any moment. If they get away from Rafinga, I think I am lost . . ." Erica's tone was frightened.

"Don't fret, Sister. I will not let that happen. I have a new ally as well—your friend Nick is with me and will do whatever is needed to find you. It is nearly dark, and the plan is for Nick to come into the village and scout for the vent you have described. Is there any way you can move it around from the bottom?" Martin asked.

"I don't think so, but let me work on it. There is no point in me shouting or screaming—apart from the soundproofing, they will hear me and come and tie and gag me," she said.

Erica looked around the cellar for the hundredth time, seeing the same crates, drums and carpets. She realised that she had not tried to open the one crate under the carpets, and started pushing the pile off onto the ground. The lid of the crate was loose and she heaved it open. It was full of camping gear, folding chairs, a table and several camp cots that have a steel rod and canvas construction, neatly rolled and tied. She puzzled over the collection for a while, not seeing any use for anything, apart from now having a comfortable chair to sit on.

"I can even make up a proper bed," she thought to herself, unwrapping one of the cots. The rods slotted into each other to extend the length down either side of the canvas sling, and an idea sprang into her mind. She slid the rods out of the pockets of all the cots until she had a collection of them piled at her feet. Joining them all together, she had a long, bendy pole that extended across the whole floor of the cellar. She moved under the vent and tried to push the rod up the pipe, but it made a terrible clanging against the galvanised steel and she froze, waiting for the scrape of the trapdoor. Withdrawing the pole, she took off both her shoes and socks and then bundled one sock into a ball and put it in the other. Sliding the sock over the end of the pole, she secured it with a shoelace and now had a padded end to her invention. It moved up the pipe almost silently, with just the occasional scrape from one of the pole joints. She pushed on until the padded end reached the vent hood.

"What now?" she asked herself. She tried turning the vent but could not tell if anything was happening, and it did not feel as if it was changing direction. She then tried pushing upwards with more strength. To her surprise, she felt the vent lifting up and realised it was probably just loosely fitted over the vent pipe, spinning smoothly on the greased rim when the wind changed.

"If I push it too far, it will come off and create a huge clatter as it falls on the tin roof," she muttered. "But I need to move it up and down enough for Martin or Nick to see . . ."

She experimented a few times, measuring the amount of lift by the number of times she changed hands as she pushed.

"About eight inches. That should be visible if someone is looking," she estimated.

Hearing movement above, Erica scrambled to disconnect the rods, throw them in the crate and pile some carpets back on the lid. She was just in time to sit down on her mattress as the trapdoor opened and the light went out. Bamjee gave her the usual instructions about facing away and keeping quiet as he dropped a fresh bottle of water and another packet of sandwiches on the floor.

"I think tonight is your last night here, Miss Granger," came the sibilant voice in the darkness. "Your Smoking Man tells me things are getting hot and it is time to move you. It will not be soon enough for me, although you have been an exemplary guest," he chuckled as he tramped back up the stairs and closed the trapdoor, leaving her breathless in the pitch darkness for a few seconds before the light came on again. She heard Bamjee talking to someone, and although the voices were muffled, she thought she recognised the other person's replies. There was something about the inflection and timbre that struck a chord. "Ngubane!" she almost screamed out loud. "Its Ngubane, I'm sure! He's come to rescue me. Maybe he is investigating Bamjee. Do I call out and let him know, or will I endanger us both?" Before she could make a decision, the voices faded and she faintly heard the front door slam, and her chance was lost. She took comfort in knowing someone was on her trail, but was terrified she had missed the only opportunity to free herself.

She sat down again and gathered her thoughts before contacting Martin with the news that she could move the roof vent up and down.

"I just hope there are not hundreds of these vents in Rafinga," she said to Martin as much to herself. "You cannot stroll around town looking at every building hoping to spot the tiny movement of one vent amongst many."

"Well, it is a plan," said Martin, "and a plan has some chance of success. Just wandering around looking for you may be futile, but this way we have a target to aim for, and I will find you."

As dusk fell, Nick returned to Martin's hideout and gave his report, saying that he had met the game reserve team and told them the elephant tracks had veered west, where there were rugged mountains and thick bush, but nobody else had used the service road.

Martin told him of the plan, half-formed, of the moving air vent and they discussed various ways of searching.

"Don't you think it is time to involve the Police and others?" asked Nick. "They can cover much more ground than us . . ."

"Not a chance," snapped Martin. "There are traitors and informants everywhere, and just having a whole lot of people blundering around might alert them and scare them into running. If we lose Erica in a car chase we may never see her again."

"But you cannot go sneaking around the village either," reasoned Nick. "No matter how quiet you are, you are going to be seen and there will be a hue and cry like this village has never seen before. I think I should be the one to scout around, looking for the vent, and then we can decide from there what to do."

They discussed the plan and agreed that it made sense for Nick to try and locate the building. They waited until the village was quiet, and then Martin contacted Erica, asking her to start pushing the vent in an hour's time. Nick walked quietly through the bush, over the railway line and into the outskirts of the village. There were enough street and window lights to see his way, but he was dismayed to find that the rooftops were in almost total darkness. He knew that it was unlikely that any of the smaller houses would have roof vents, and in his mind's eye, he recalled only seeing them on commercial buildings and farm barns.

"So, I'll concentrate on the shopping area first and then move to the light industrial and storage streets behind the town," he made his plan. He was stepping backwards into the middle of the street in an attempt to get a better view of the roofs on the main street when a heavy hand fell on his shoulder from behind.

"What are you up to, young man?" growled a deep voice as a powerful torch flashed in his face. Nick nearly collapsed in fright and could not speak for a few seconds. He recognised the Police uniform and stuttered, "Sorr-sorry sir, we have lost our parrot and I am looking for him."

It sounded pathetic, even to himself, but the Constable seemed to have bitten.

"But you are from the farm, not town. What is your parrot doing here?" He was no fool.

"We brought him into town for the vet to clip his nails and beak again. He hates it and somehow got away. My mom will kill me if I don't find him," Nick warmed to his story.

"Well, you are not going to get far without a torch, are you?" pointed out the policeman. "Come back to the station with me and I'll see if I can rustle up a spare one for you."

Nick was limp with fear and relief, and left the Constable with a promise to return the torch before his shift was up. The missing parrot was duly entered into the charge office Occurrence Book with a note to keep an eye out for an irritated African Grey called Polly.

Nick resumed his search of the main store buildings with no success and then moved to the back streets where the welding workshops, old tyre traders and others plied their businesses. He did see some vents, but none of them either moved or indicated the type of building they were looking for.

Erica was becoming exhausted, pushing the heavy rods up and down was draining on her arm and wrist muscles, and her back was cramping. It did not, however, stop her from carrying on. She felt it was her last chance.

Nick was becoming desperate, and started back for the centre of the village, walking by chance down the street where Bamjee's store was. He happened to glance down the alley between the store and the next building, and just caught a glance of light shining on the fin of a roof vent on the far side of a building at the end of the alley. Pressing himself against the wall of the alley, he waited and watched for any sign of movement before creeping softly towards the building, which he realised as a house front. Light shone dimly through yellowed curtains. A yapping dog startled him until he realised it was at least a street away.

Because of the angle of the roof, Nick could not see the whole vent, just the fin that crested it. He watched it intently, seeing no movement at all, and was crushed by the feeling they were losing the game. He was about to turn away when he thought he saw a slight movement of the fin. Yes! Almost imperceptibly it was moving up and down, just a few inches, but now unmistakeable, catching a glint of streetlight every few seconds.

Nick ran all the way back to the Police Station, thanked the constable on duty for the torch, reported that Polly was under lock and key, and then made his way back to Martin, stumbling occasionally in the darkness. Martin heard him coming long before he got there, and had retreated even further back into the tangled undergrowth in case it was not him.

"Martin!" Nick called urgently. "Are you there? We've found her!"

Martin's heart swelled in joy.

"Well done, lad. Well done!" he touched Nick on the shoulder with his trunk.

"Erica. Erica, you can stop pushing. Put that stuff away, we have found you!" called Martin to the exhausted prisoner. "We will be there at first light, be prepared for us."

Erica slumped down to the floor, hardly believing her ordeal may be ending. After a while she recovered and repacked everything that she had disturbed, tidying up her cell and replacing the vent cover. She put on her shoes and socks and prepared herself for anything that might happen.

Martin and Nick discussed their strategy for the rescue, and it came down to Martin's choice of blunt and massive force. He realised there was no way they could sneak into town without a huge furore which might give the Smoking Man a chance to still get Erica away. The best was a very fast charge straight into the middle of it all. Before anybody would have a chance to gather their thoughts, they should be in and out. Martin also realised that he was probably going to be shot, not by the kidnappers, but frightened villagers or the Police or both.

They passed the hours until dawn reassuring each other and trying to find loopholes in the plan, simple as it was.

Just before the first tinge of light showed to the east, the unlikely pair set off for the village, Nick leading the way. It was dead quiet, with only a sleepy rooster tuning up his morning call somewhere, and the isolated yap of a distant dog. Quiet that is, until they got to Bamjee's store. A car was parked in the alley, facing towards the street with the parking lights on. The boot was open, as was the front door to the house.

Angry voices could be heard from inside, and once, Martin thought he heard Erica sob. It was plain that they had come to take her away, and a red mist descended over his mind. With a blast of sound between a trumpet and a squeal, he launched forward, ears wide and trunk over the shoulder. As Martin crashed into the front of the house, Nick dashed forward and reached into the car, ripping the keys from the ignition and throwing them as far as he could. Martin stood back a few paces and again charged into the flimsy wood and galvanised iron wall, splintering and buckling it as if an avalanche had fallen upon the house. Nick could hear Bamjee screaming and another man cursing as their world collapsed around them.

Suddenly, a man appeared at the remains of the door, holding Erica roughly by the neck, a pistol at her head. Despite the early morning darkness, he had on reflective dark glasses.

"Whatever the hell is going on out here, if you don't stop, she dies!" yelled the Smoking Man, seeing for the first time Martin towering over him. The Smoking Man nearly lost his nerve but then thought to himself, "I've shot plenty of your sort before, my friend. You don't scare me."

Martin shook his head in frustration and lunged forward, stopping as he saw the tightening of the trigger finger, realising that this man would carry out his threat.

The Smoking Man edged towards the car, keeping Erica between him and Martin, pushing her across into the passenger seat before jumping in and slamming the door. He reached for the ignition key and cursed when he found it gone. It took him seconds to remember he always kept a spare under the dashboard, and fumbled for it, all the while keeping the ugly black snout of the pistol on Erica.

As he started the car, a young man rushed out of the darkness and reached through the window for the key. With one swift movement, the Smoking Man swiped Nick across the face with the pistol, sending him reeling back, blood pouring down into his eyes. Martin once again started forward, but the Smoking Man gestured at Erica with the pistol extended towards her, his face twisted in hate and frustration, and Martin hesitated.

The car, wheels spitting gravel, started down the alley towards the street and Martin knew he had lost the race. Suddenly, a figure stepped into the alley, pistol raised and calmly shot out the two front tyres, stepping away as the car sideswiped towards him and then shooting the rear tyre for good measure. The man then lunged for the driver's door, wrenching it open and dragging the Smoking Man out in what seemed like one fluid movement.

"Erica! Get out of the car and lie down!" Mufara's voice was loud and commanding as he tried to take the pistol from the Smoking Man's iron grip. They were engaged in a bizarre dance, with each holding on to the other's pistol hand, but Mufara was outweighed by the huge thug. Martin recovered and came rushing forward just as the Smoking Man wrenched his gun hand free and brought the muzzle to bear on Mufara's chest. Martin squealed again, and the Smoking Man took one look at the charging beast and loosed off two shots. The bullets thudded into Martin's chest, but he did not even hesitate as he reached out in blind anger. Mufara staggered back as the muzzle flashes seared his face and Martin snared Smoking Man's wrist in his trunk. He jerked the man off his feet so hard, the sound of his arm dislocating could be clearly heard above all the noise. He screamed in pain and dropped the pistol. Martin put him back on the ground, almost gently, and then delicately removed the dark glasses that had survived the events of the past few seconds.

"So, that is the face of evil," he said quietly. "I thought it would be far more impressive . . ."

The Smoking Man thought he was hallucinating in his pain, but Mufara, also recovering his eyesight, heard or felt the words and was stunned.

"This is for Erica, and for my family and for any other animal you have made suffer," Martin said as he wrapped his trunk around the neck of the Smoking Man and threw him against the alley wall. As he bounced back, sprawling on the ground, Martin knelt on his chest, ribs audibly popping and crackling like some obscene breakfast cereal.

"That's for hitting a child in the face," he grunted, now feeling some pain from the bullets lodged deep in his chest. "And this, this is because I really don't like you at all," lifting the Smoking Man by one leg, Martin spun him around like a rag doll and then tossed him high into the morning sky. The Smoking Man crashed down on the sharp edge of the vent fin of Erica's prison and lay impaled there, motionless.

Erica came stumbling around the side of the car, wrists still tied with plastic bands, tears coursing down her dirty cheeks.

"Oh Martin, you came! Nick, you came!' she cried. "And Mufara, I don't know who you are or what you are doing, but you saved my life!"

Mufara slipped a knife out of his pocket and cut the ties before heading towards the shattered remains of Bamjee's front wall to see what had happened to the old rogue.

By this time, the whole village was astir and gathering at the end of the alley. The police arrived in force, but were held back by the sight of a huge bull elephant being held by two children, a shot-up car, destroyed building and the distant sight of a man apparently sleeping on a roof vent.

All the rumours were true! Rafinga was the centre of everything this morning and would never be the same. They would be famous!

Rob Granger, alerted by the sound of gunfire, arrived quickly and pushed through the throng. He was amazed by the sight of his daughter, alive and well, stroking the trunk of a very large bull elephant in the middle of a quiet country village, but took it in his stride, hugging her close with tears running down his face.

"Oh, Dad!" she cried, "I thought I'd never see you again. I love you so much. I'm sorry I caused you so much pain."

"You cause me nothing but pleasure in your being alive, Erica," he muttered, stroking her hair back gently. "But will somebody tell me what is going on here?"

"Dad, this is my brother, Martin. The first thing we need is a doctor—he has two bullets in his chest. They are small pistol bullets, but they must be taken out before they become infected."

Granger looked at the wounds and agreed that they were not life-threatening in the hard muscle of the chest but needed attention.

"Let's get him down to the veterinary surgery," he said. "I'm sure the vet will love this one and put it in his life story!"

They set off down the alley, people scattering before them like chaff in the wind. Nick started to go along with them, but Granger asked one of the Police team to take him to the clinic to have the gash in his head seen to.

"We'll pick you up later, Nick," Granger promised. "I assume you are going to be in a spot of bother with your dad over this?"

Nick smiled through the drying blood on his face.

"Worth every minute, sir. I'd do it again in a flash."

A commotion behind them made them stop and turn. Mufara had emerged from the battered house with a rumpled Bamjee in handcuffs stumbling before him, gabbling excuses and protesting his innocence.

"Save it for the judge, Bamjee. This time you are really going down. I am so glad you kidnapped Erica, because we won't even have to worry about the poaching and dealing charges. You are toast."

Erica came up to Mufara. "Thank you Mufara, I will never be able to say how much. Where is Ngubane, he must be working with you. I heard his voice last night."

"I am really sorry to tell you that your mole was Ngubane," Mufara paused while Erica gasped and Granger recoiled. "He has expensive tastes and aspirations. Being a senior warden is not amongst them. He also got himself entangled with Mugani, Erica's Smoking Man, some time back, and couldn't have redeemed himself even if he wanted to, which I am sure he did from time to time."

"Where is he?" asked Granger before Erica could pose the same question.

"I'm afraid I've lost him for the time being," replied Mufara. "I think he caught onto me before I could close that particular net, and in any event, Mugani and Bamjee were my primary targets. Taking Erica was their biggest mistake. I could not let the operation spin out any more after that, and getting her back was the only priority. Ngubane will turn up in the fullness of time."

He turned away and started off towards the Police Station with Bamjee in tow, still whining and pleading.

The vet was suitably impressed, if a little intimidated by carrying out an operation on an elephant still awake and grumpy, in the front garden of his house attached to the surgery.

"Yes, well, a little too large to jump up on the old examining table, eh?" He tried his best bedside manner under the trying conditions.

"Just get on with it," rumbled Martin." I am tired, I want to go home and you people wear me down with your endless chat chat chat. And by the way, I do NOT want to become a sensation because I can communicate with you. I will not submit to any tests, be anybody's experiment or otherwise cooperate. If you do not agree, I will disappear and you will never see me again."

Erica went white at that, and stared at Martin, who turned his head away from the others and gave her a big, slow wink.

Postscript

The poaching teams, standing by for Mugani's orders outside the reserve, were mopped up and prosecuted with evidence provided by Mufara.

Mugani's army accomplices were arrested and charged under military law.

Mugani, well, he got his just desserts.

Ngubane was caught trying to cross the border into South Africa dressed as a pregnant woman.

He was charged with various offences, and is awaiting conviction.

Bamjee was convicted of a string of crimes, the worst being the abduction of a minor with intent to extort.

He is a guest of the State for the next fifteen years.

Nick van Heerden was soundly rebuked by his father, who then hugged him and called him a real man.

And started treating him like one.

Erasmus found his 'big' gun and awaits the next invasion. He has forgotten where the bullets are.

Rob Granger is looking for another mechanic. And continues the battle against poachers.

Martin was appointed Guardian of the Graveyard and takes his duties seriously.

Mufara is in New York, tracking down a syndicate selling dried Pangolin parts.

Erica is back at school. She and Nick are an 'item'. Who knows where that might end . . .

The End